Library and Archives Canada Cataloguing in Publication

Butler, Paul, 1964-
  NaGeira : a novel / Paul Butler.

ISBN 1-894463-89-7

1. Women--Newfoundland and Labrador--Fiction. 2. Women--Ireland--Fiction.
3. Newfoundland and Labrador--Fiction. 4. Mythology, Celtic--Fiction. I. Title.

PS8553.U735N33 2006   C813'.6   C2006-901040-4

Copyright © 2006 by Paul Butler

PRINTED IN CANADA

*BRAZEN BOOKS and PENNYWELL BOOKS
are imprints of Flanker Press Ltd.*

FLANKER PRESS
ST. JOHN'S, NL, CANADA
TOLL FREE: 1-866-739-4420
WWW.FLANKERPRESS.COM

COVER ART: ADAM FREAKE

First Canadian edition printed April 2006

10 9 8 7 6 5 4 3 2 1

Canada   Canada Council Conseil des Arts
             for the Arts   du Canada

We acknowledge the financial support of: the Government of Canada through the Book Publishing Industry Development Program (BPIDP); the Canada Council for the Arts which last year invested $20.3 million in writing and publishing throughout Canada; the Government of Newfoundland and Labrador, Department of Tourism, Culture and Recreation.

A NOVEL

PENNYWELL BOOKS
ST. JOHN'S, NL
2006

To P.D. and H.B.

"Hark, in thine ear: change places; and, handy-dandy, which is the justice, which is the thief?"

William Shakespeare

CHAPTER ONE

There is another creak from the threshold. I glance from the table and see the sunlight harsh upon the floor's shrunken planks. The door, wide open, hides whoever is too shy to approach.

"Come!" I say, my voice no more than a croak.

No answer.

A couple of dry pine needles scatter along the floor as the breeze changes direction. "Is that you, David Butt?" Though no one shows himself, I can think of no other who would stand on a doorstep trying to gather courage. I have observed David Butt well and know he is nearing his changes. His eyes are restless, and his skin turns red with no warning as though all the secrets burning inside him might spill out at any moment and splash onto the floor.

I go back to work, wrenching the black feathers from the still-warm crow's carcass. The creaking comes again, and suddenly

1

David does appear, his fair hair thicker than autumn straw, his cheeks as red as apples.

"Why didn't you answer me, boy?" My voice is sharp, though I am not really angry.

His green eyes glisten like those of a rabbit sensing a danger it does not understand.

"Answer?" he says. He turns back toward the doorway as though expecting to see someone else there. "Answer to what?"

My hands cease working. David stares down at the half-plucked bird, the pile of black feathers, and my pink swollen fingers flecked with blood. Most people would be disgusted, but this boy's eyes are as curious as those of a babe who looks for the first time upon the rich dome of a summer sky.

"How long were you standing outside building up courage to enter?" I ask.

The boy hesitates, half-turns, then blinks.

"I just got here."

He looks so startled I don't have the heart to argue.

"I've been down by the wharf unloading with Uncle Seth. I was thinking about it, though, thinking of asking you . . . something . . ." The boy stumbles over his words. His cheeks flush.

Men begin where women end, it seems. My face burned like his thirty years ago to mark the end of my regenerative years. It ended in fire. I could feel it crackling within me. *Go to sleep, old woman*, said the hiss and snap of the rising heat. Your time to teem children has gone. Now, as the sap rises in this young man, a similar heat scolds him. Fiery shadows distract his sleep and enter his dreams. He wonders if he will ever feel comfortable and composed again, so overpowering is the great itch rising within him.

I watch him stutter once more and feel a smile upon my lips. I can't help it. The arrogance of youth amuses me. He is the first boy ever to feel as he does, and he guards it all—this great secret. He feels that if someone were to catch one glimpse into his heart it would surely send cracks through the earth and bring about the Apocalypse.

"Who do you want to lay with, child?" I say casually.

His eyes open wide and his mouth gapes. His feet shuffle backwards and he flinches as though struck. "It's not that!" he says firmly.

"No?"

"No, not the way you think," he huffs, his mouth and eyes suddenly moist.

"The way I think?"

"It's respect," he says, taking a step to one side, flapping his arms. At first he looks as if he will lecture me like his Uncle Seth, pacing the room, a pipe in his mouth. Then he stops, looks fearful and adds more quietly. "It is honour and regard I wish to convey to . . . someone." He hesitates, looking down at the floor, lip trembling. "And the same that I wish to receive in return."

"If it's words you wish for, you seem to have them already," I say, trying not to smile too broadly. "Such words become a young gentleman as truly as finest silks, as true as sword and polished scabbard, as true as golden carriage and shining white horse. Why do you not go straight to this young lady with your fine words?"

The boy stares back at me, his mouth tight as though sewn shut, his eyes angry.

"I know why you won't," I continue. "It's because the words only tell half the story. You are afraid if you open your mouth to your young lady to give them utterance, these words will betray you. You will try to say these high-minded things, but your tongue will trip and spill the other half of the story instead, the part you wish to keep concealed."

The boy sighs, exasperated. He raises his arms again and makes a face a man might make under torture. "Why do you make everything so . . ."

"Truthful?"

The boy grunts, resentful but not arguing, and sits down on a joint-stool close to my working table.

"I want her to feel as I do," he mumbles defeated, scuffing his boots against the floor. "I want her to notice me as I notice her."

"Sara Rose?"

He blinks, astonished.

"How do you know?"

"Even I hear the best-known gossip. She may not have noticed you, my boy, but everyone has noticed you noticing her."

Helplessly I watch his face form into a desperate frown. A shipwrecked man watching his wife, mother, child, and all his possessions pulled into the black, hissing waves of a storm could not have looked more forlorn.

"Now what chance do I have?" he cries from somewhere deep inside himself.

He looks so raw and shocked—like a hare that has been skinned in its sleep and awakes to see itself bloody and steaming in the reflection of a pond. I feel I must comfort him.

"Perhaps not everyone knows," I offer a little doubtfully.

The boy gives a short, mirthless laugh and stares at the floor again. "But *she* must know," he murmurs.

"But what does it matter if she does?" There is a sudden impatience in my voice. No one takes himself more seriously than a young man in love, and this morose child is wearing me down. "You may not have noticed it, young man, but there are few enough of us in this little place. Get it off your chest, boy, and move on if she refuses you. Move on before her sisters are spoken for, too."

"Sisters!" The boy almost spits.

"You'll be mourning over one of her sisters like a lovesick calf before the end of this summer if the first one refuses you."

"It's not like that. Not with me."

"Not with you, ah." My fingers are working with the crow again, plucking carefully, stopping every time the boy speaks.

Now he looks up at me, curious.

"What are the feathers for?"

"Your Uncle Seth. Newly plucked crow feathers will ease the stiffness in his shoulder."

His green eyes watch my bloody fingers.

"How do you know what works and what doesn't?"

He hunches his shoulders and scuffs his boots on the plank flooring again.

I allow myself another smile and pluck the last few feathers from the bird. Its bald, pink head twists dejected on the table as its body jolts to the action of my fingers.

"What you really want to ask," I say, "is how do I know a love spell will work if I prepare one for you."

I lift the crow's carcass by the wing and hold it out to the boy. "Throw this to your uncle's dogs. When I have prepared his medicine, I will see to yours."

The boy springs to his feet, grabs the bird, and flies out of the door as weightless as if he has inherited the former life of the unhappy creature he carries.

————

"We burn something of yours and something of hers together in the same flame."

David still holds his palm to the side of his head as though stemming the bloodflow from a mortal wound.

"Come," I say. "It could not have hurt so much and you have plenty to spare."

"You could have used a knife rather than pulling from the root!"

"And lose precious skin and blood?" I say, laying the clump of coarse sandy hair close by the now raging hearth. The wood the boy brought me is good and dry and will do for days. It hisses and smokes but little, sending odd sparks rising into the room. They waver in mid-air for a moment, then wink out in the darkness. The nights are still cold, and I am getting too old now to gather wood for myself.

"What do you have of hers?" he says hugging himself morosely, sitting far off by the joint-stool.

I reach into the folds of my dress and pull out the tooth—dried blood still on the root and a crack down the middle. "When you are physician to everyone, a piece of everyone remains with you."

His look of disgust does not affect the odd sense of pride I feel. No one in this place can do without me, I know. It doesn't matter how I am shunned. Sudden elation gets the better of me for a moment and I am like a child again, striking out for the first time to discover the possibilities and limitations of my powers. I defy the crone that has become my outward shell. It is just a disguise; I can feel the withering years peeling away from me. "You should be careful what you wish for, my boy," I say. "A girl who loses a first tooth at thirteen will likely lose her last at twenty. You will feel you are sucking on the mouth of a codfish!" I laugh with abandon. Although it feels like the mirth of youth flowing in a torrent, I'm sure the boy, who now purses his lips and turns to the door, would call it a cackle.

He knows he cannot leave now. His desire is too great and is held fast in my darkened room as sure as the black and gold shadows that leap and duck over the four walls.

"Now come, boy, kneel beside me by the fire."

I turn to the flames with the boy's hair in one hand, the tooth of his beloved in the other. He leaves the joint-stool and shuffles towards me, kneeling.

"What now?" he says.

"Put out your hand as though to receive."

Obediently he does so. I put the clump of his hair in the middle of his palm. His hand is sweating and the hair sticks as it should. I place the tooth in the centre of this little nest.

"Now close your fist."

Again he does as he's told.

"Now," I say grabbing hold of his wrist and turning it so that the knuckles face upward. I can feel his alarm in the stiffness of his hand. "Don't be afraid. Hold on as long as you can. Only when you cannot bear it any longer, only then can you open your fist and let the hair and the tooth drop on the fire."

Feeling his wrist tug away, I look at him hard. His eyes glisten with fear and he is breathing quickly, yet I know he is bracing himself. He nods. I put both my hands behind his elbow. David grits his teeth and mumbles to himself. I squeeze his elbow tight as a sign to get ready, then push his elbow forward. He does not resist.

David gives a muffled cry and jolts his arm back for a moment. Stiffening, he plunges it forward again, gives a small, rising moan but keeps his fist steady above the flame. Then, shaking with pain, he opens his fist and pulls his hand away, cradling it to his belly like a chick he has lost and found again.

The hair and tooth land on a glowing log. The hair sizzles and curls around Sara's tooth. A single small flame dances around, licking the now black and withering strands. *Perfect!*

The boy shivers and breathes heavily, his head bowed.

"Up!" I say, using my knuckles against his shoulders to climb into a standing position. He is slow to react. "Salt water!" I say to rouse him. "And quickly, or your hand will be useless for a week."

I lift the bucket onto the table while he gradually rises, stumbles towards the table, and plunges his hand into the water. He cries out, turning his head to the ceiling, eyes tight shut.

"Quiet!" I hiss at him. "Do you want them to hear you down in the cove?"

I know no one will hear us—my home is far from the rest of the settlement. But this boy is beginning to worry me. So timid, yet sullen; so backward with his girl, yet so determined to win her, no matter how singed his skin must become in the attempt.

"If your uncle, or anyone else, asks about your burn, tell them you were helping me with the fire."

The boy doesn't reply but looks down, drawing his hand out of the bucket. Tears of pain run down his face and he breathes hard, gritting his teeth.

"What now?" David asks, gazing down at his pink and trembling hand.

"Now?"

"What must I do to win her?"

"You have done it already. Go home. Rest. Let the medicine work."

He stands rigid, still staring into his quivering palm as though expecting to see some kind of answer there.

"You have sent your message to the gods and goddesses who reign over all," I whisper to comfort him. "They are in all living things, in the earth and the sky. You have joined Sara and yourself in the flames. To the gods, you are one."

"What if it doesn't work?" says the boy, his tears mingling with sweat.

"It will work because the spirits move in Sara as they move in us all."

The boy stares at me for a second.

"I am grateful to you, Sheila," he says, then turns for the door.

"Treat her well if you want to repay me."

He nods without turning. His movements are slower, heavier than before. I think of the boy who came to see me earlier, his coltish love and his shyness. That boy was a more delicate creature altogether than the figure whose shoulders now block my narrow doorway.

David opens the door and steps into the night, closing it after him with a clunk. His heavy footfalls crunch on the path as he makes his way down to the cove.

I turn back to the fire which still leaps and ducks around the wood. The spitting violence of the flames seems meant for me, but I am equal to it and stare back in defiance. We are adversaries, the fire and I, and I do not mean to yield to it yet.

CHAPTER TWO

I have lived too long, and I know it. It's been part of me always, this inclination to survive. All my life I have been skipping rocks over a writhing ocean. People around me gurgle and scream, their anguish like wasps in my ears, but my nimble feet carry me along, barely allowing for pause. As I am predestined to outlast them, I feel a passing sorrow, but little guilt. I have lived beyond events which should wring the very soul from a woman. I have heard the cries of my children as they are taken or slain by pirates, and have felt the fire of grief overcome me. Salt tears have turned my cheeks to rivers. My very life, it seems, oozed in that flow, mingling with the dust at my feet.

But the salt tears dried upon my face, crusted, turned to powder. I was breathing, seeing, feeling. Before too long even hunger began to nibble at my ribs. I would go in search of food to sustain myself. What manner of thing am I to have survived so much?

But I knew from the start. I had been warned.

11

When I was a child, I met the man of the forest. I recall but little of his appearance now. It was a face that revealed itself one moment, then faded the next into shifting light and shadow. A face whose contours were the knots and dips of tree bark. I remember how his voice hissed gently like the rustling of leaves. *The forest is yours,* he said, through the whispering melodies of the foliage. *While the woods embrace you, no spirit or beast can harm you, no strangers or neighbours smite you, no dank ague infect you. When death lies all around you, the leaves and boughs protect you.*

I cannot justify or explain it even to myself—this feeling that the lives are too fleeting to mourn, that only the heart of the forest is constant. I met a playwright once in a London prison. Much of what he said seemed nonsense, but one thing, I thought, was quite good. He talked of life as a flame. "Out brief candle," he said.

It stuck with me.

———

If only they knew, the people who live in the cove, how easy it is to grow old. I see them studying me sometimes, trying to fathom my secrets. Like cats watching the surface of a stream for movement, they imagine they will catch some word, some action that might explain it to them. *That's it,* they might say, *she crosses her legs from right to left, this is why she has grown wise enough to overcome the frailty of years.* Or, *I know! She bathes her forehead in brine twice a day. That's how she keeps time's scimitar at bay.*

It's the one thing they respect me for, my age. They accept my cures grudgingly. They even listen to my stories with half an ear. But somewhere deep in their hearts, they distrust me. They look to the ocean and build their homes close to its dim and murmuring shores. I look to the woods where I feel protected by the birds and the fragrance of pine.

My age is the least of me. They can have it.

I used to think I was lucky. I used to think that was what the man of the forest was telling me. But I was a child then and that is how a child hears things. The bough is always heavy with fruit, the meadow always sweet, the cheek always flushed with hope and belief. I was coiled like a young fern, ready for and fully expectant of happiness.

My father was born in Ireland, just outside the Pale, but he had lived in England for three years by the time I was born. Soon after, when I was still very small, we returned to Ireland, to live within the Pale among the other English. "I am the Queen's subject now," he told my mother. "As are you and Sheila. It is the way things will be in Ireland from now on. If our monarch can beat back the Spanish, she can surely tame the bogs of this heathen land."

I have never seen so much green as when our ship landed. The sea was the colour of a meadow after a June rain, and the hills and woods were pulsing with life. I swore I saw them growing before my eyes. My father was to be one of most prosperous landowners of the Pale, that part of Ireland "to which civilization had already come," as he used to say. The rest, we were told, was a dark place from which we needed protection. The snakes had all gone in St. Patrick's time, but vagabonds, beggars, and wild men roamed the forests with clubs and knives, ready to pounce. Here in the Pale, though, my father had a hundred and twenty sheep and fields that rolled to the horizon. I would climb the tallest tree and gaze at the ocean of green before me—my father's kingdom, I thought. The mingling scents of pine and ash and oak made me dizzy. I breathed in the slippery moss on my hands and felt something swell in my chest. I knew there were murmurings even in the Pale about father being a traitor. Beyond the English territories the wild men would tear him apart. But the militia protected us here, just as in centuries long past the legions of Rome had protected the outposts of the great Empire. This is what my father used to say. England, in time, would be the new Rome. Queen Bess was our Julius.

Sometimes I wasn't sure where I was living. "Is this place England then, or is it Rome?" I asked my mother as she wove by the hearth. "Neither," she would say quietly with a smile, touching her bottom lip with her tongue as she concentrated on her sewing. "This is Ireland but we are under the protectorship of England, which is, in some ways, like Rome."

I still had no idea where Ireland lay. But wherever it was, it was my home and I loved it. I had no notion ever to leave.

———

Then one day everything changed. I was nestled high in my tree watching swallows dart in and out of the ocean of leaves below. The sky was like blue crystal and there was nothing between it and me. The sun pulsed its warmth onto my upturned face, and the breeze scattered its music among the foliage.

Suddenly I was jolted from the top branches by a shriek—it pierced like a sword through the fabric of the afternoon before trailing away into something quieter but no less desperate-sounding. It was then, as it calmed from its animal fury, that I recognized the voice of my mother. I felt the rumble of horses from the earth below.

Like a rock scrambling down a cliff face, I scuffed my way to the forest floor. I ripped through the woods towards my home, snagging my clothes, ducking the boughs, and dodging the tree stumps I had grown to know as friends. Different faces—frowning and serious—now formed in the twisted bark; a wrinkled brow here, an open mouth there.

I came into the clearing in front of our house, surprised somehow to see its red bricks still standing, its roof showing no smoke or fire. Two of my father's men, Michael and William, were standing outside the front door. Michael caught my eye and looked away. William shuffled his feet and kept his gaze on the ground. Breathless, I scambled between them and into the house.

Inside, my father was laid out on the floor. His eyes were open, staring at the ceiling. Mother paced, wringing her hands, breathing hard. She gasped when she saw me, swooped upon me, squeezed me hard, pressing her fingers into my shoulders. "Little one, little one," was all she said. Her voice was strange and seemed to come from another world. Then, just as quickly, she left me, clasping her hands once more and circling my father.

———

The man of the forest had betrayed me, I thought. He had promised to take care of things. But my father was dead, pulled from his horse and stabbed by murderers, and all this happened at the very edge of the wood, the place where we should feel most protected. But then I realized the spirit's promise was narrower than I had hoped. It was a promise for me alone: it did not extend to my family.

My mother became like a ghost, white-faced and twitching. She sat in the shadows, staring into nowhere, doing little in those first few weeks after my father's death. She hardly spoke to the servants, though they often came before her asking questions in soft voices, bowing when she waved them away. Then one day I saw her through the open door of the study. She was at my father's writing desk, scratching intently with a quill. She stared so hard at the parchment upon which she worked that I thought she must be coming out of her daze. But as soon as she gave it to the boy, Samuel, to arrange delivery, she fell back into silence.

My uncle James came to the house regularly now with his wife. He stood in the centre of the room with his hands behind his back, tutted at my mother, pointed occasionally at me and shook his head. Gazing at the ceiling, he talked, to no one in particular, of how he must now stay and oversee the farm. He was a big man with shoulders like a bull, and small dark eyes that always seemed to be swimming in liquid. He wiped them often with his handkerchief so that anyone who did not know better would think he was wiping away tears of grief.

One day, when my uncle was with us, the sheriff arrived. He had come before but had been sent away by my mother. This time he was more successful, making it to the entranceway of the dining hall where my mother had received guests after the wake. He was a finely dressed gentleman who smelled of pomade. His grey eyes glistened with intensity when he talked about the Crown and taxes and such things that held no interest to me. I wanted my mother to tell him to leave, but she merely bowed her head. He seemed sharp like a bad-tempered fox as he snapped at her, in a voice far too loud, that if he left empty-handed the property and lands would be forfeit to the Crown.

Who was this man to threaten my mother? I thought. We had owned the house and the grounds for years now. Why did neither she nor my uncle tell him to leave? I put my hands over my ears and retreated to a corner.

Though tight-lipped and defiant, the sheriff had an anxious air. He fingered his hat and blinked too often, like a man trying to outface the sun. He and my uncle began to argue. Their voices were like barn doors banging in the wind, the same words repeated over and over with increased emphasis. But like a wind, the argument at last began to calm. It became a discussion. Glances were thrown at my mother and aunt who were sitting together by the window, my aunt weaving, my mother just staring through the glass. Before long the two men retreated to the study where, unbeknownst to them, I had escaped a moment earlier. Even though they thought they were alone their voices were still soft, just above a whisper. They need not have worried about me even if they had been aware I was crouched under my father's old desk. I understood nothing of deeds, Crown rights, and commissions.

When the sheriff and my uncle left the room, I followed. I watched the sheriff give my mother a paper and tell her he would return the following week. If she could not make arrangements for the property's transference to a suitable owner, he said, he would be forced to take possession. Then he looked meaningfully at my uncle who bent over and whispered quietly to her. He motioned his wife to join him, and told my mother he would return in a few days.

Mother continued to stare out of the window until they were long gone.

———

The next time we heard the grind of hooves on the pathway, it was neither my uncle nor the sheriff. My mother was at her place by the window. She turned sharply when she heard the sound and—I could hardly believe it—like a statue imbued with sudden life, she picked up her skirts and ran to the door.

At first I thought my father had returned. The soft voice of the man of the forest seemed to whisper in my ear once more. Was my father's death merely a trick which could be righted? Was I like the child whose parent pretends to forget her birthday only so that he may sweep her from sorrow to dizzying joy in a moment? I remembered how my father's eyes were still open even though everyone told me he was gone. If they are open, I had thought, then they can still see. And now it seemed I had been right all along!

I ran after my mother and held onto her skirts as she opened the door and leaned half-fainting against the entranceway. Afraid to look as the footsteps grew louder, I bit my lip and felt her lean forward. I opened my eyes to see her holding out her hands like two flowers to the rising sun.

It was not my father, but an English gentleman, Mr. Ridley. He had been to our house many times before and flown falcons with my father. My mother's hands fell gently into his. I took in his alien scent—a rich, mysterious cocktail of man. A feather wavered in Mr. Ridley's hat and his grey eyes fixed upon my mother so intently it seemed they would burn her through. I looked over his shoulder feeling this could not be all, that Father must be some way behind him.

———

Mr. Ridley was a widower. He must have been about forty years old but the lines on his face, as deep and unmoving as grooves in iron, made him seem much older. He was a landowner in the Pale but spent much of his time in England, where he made cannons, cannonballs, muskets, and bullets. He used to bring his weapons when he visited my father and they would go into the woods together to fire them at the trees or the birds. My father forbade me the woods whenever Mr. Ridley was staying. From the house I could hear the *crack-crack* of pistol fire and the collective shriek of scattering birds. I remembered wondering why men can never be peaceful, why their progress anywhere was always accompanied by gunfire or loud, mirthless laughter. I didn't like Mr. Ridley and I didn't like my father as much as usual when he was with Mr. Ridley. But the day when he came to our house to comfort my mother I had never before seen Mr. Ridley look so kind.

Mother and he were drinking each other in, their fingertips touching one another's sleeves like hesitant petals. I was bursting with the riddle of my father yet afraid to speak.

A movement on the gravel near Mr. Ridley's carriage distracted me. Someone else had alighted on the opposite side. My heart beat faster and, like a whirl of scattering butterflies, joy returned to my chest. But the butterflies ceased and crumbled into powder. It was Mr. Ridley's son, Thomas. He gazed at me blankly with watery blue eyes while he gathered the horses' reins and tied them to the tree stub by the path. I watched him, my chest still heaving, my senses still strewn on the gravel of the path. He was a tall, lean boy a couple of years older than me. He had red lips and long hair the colour of sand. I had seen him before and thought nothing; I could not tell why this time was so different, but it was. My heart was plummeting, falling deeper and deeper into some black space with no bottom. Yet, even so, the sight of this boy—the way his Adam's apple bulged as he unbridled the horses, the way his sandy hair waved in the breeze then flopped back down upon his head—set off some faint bell, some faraway cathedral peal whose sweetness held me suspended.

Nothing could erase my sorrow that Father would never return. Nothing could calm my disquiet at my mother's excitement now upon seeing Mr. Ridley. But already, the boy before me had given me something to rival despair. Already, I feared less the black space through which my heart was falling. It seemed that grief might find a safer place to land.

CHAPTER THREE

A knock on the door invades my dream. Shaking Thomas Ridley from me—his red lips, and watery eyes, his coarse, sandy hair and mossy odour—I turn on the straw and rise. The ten, twenty, thirty thousand days standing between Thomas Ridley and me scatter like grains of salt as my feet touch the floor. Only a faint light struggles through the single shutter in the wall, but I know it is morning. The fire is long out and I am chilled to the bone.

I stand with effort and reach for the shutter. Pulling it open by the iron hook to admit the morning, I hear the knock again and make my way to the door. I can already imagine David Butt shuffling his feet on the other side, frantic that the spell has not yet taken effect. I pull the door open at last and take a moment to adjust.

It's not David. It's Elizabeth Rose, Sara's mother. Her eyes are alive with anxiety, her gaze darting down to the cove as though she is afraid to be seen here. She is shrunken into herself like a woman seeking to be invisible, hands crossed in front of her waist. Before I have had time to back away, she steps over the threshold, giving one last furtive glance at the settlement below as she enters the shadow of my cabin.

"I need your help, Sheila," she whispers.

My heart is racing. Does she know what I have done regarding David Butt and her daughter? Is Sara at this very moment lying in the arms of that unpromising youth, driving her mother here to make me untangle them?

"What? What's happened?" I ask rather too suddenly.

Elizabeth glances at me and wets her bottom lip with her tongue. Her face seems reptilian in its small, rapid movements. She takes a step forward and reaches out her hand to touch my arm.

"Sheila, you're the only one with the knowledge to help me."

"What knowledge?" I ask rigid with guilt.

Elizabeth's eyes soften into an appeal.

"Please," she says. "You remember when Mary was born?"

"I remember."

My heart begins to calm. This is clearly about something else.

"Do you remember Simon's disappointment," she asks, searching my face, "at not being given a son, I mean?"

"You *told* me about it, yes."

I remember nothing first hand, I feel like saying, because I was not allowed to come near you, not during the worst time when you were stuck in your home. I nursed Elizabeth's distemper only when she was strong enough to come to me. Even then, her husband, Simon Rose, would have stopped her visits had he known.

But I need not say it. Elizabeth turns from me, shamefaced, acknowledging the past. Her eyes scan my shelves and beams, the dry worms hanging from a nail, the stacks of juniper and spruce bark, the caribou moss, and the various small jars of feathers and dried innards. "Three times blessed, Sheila, and three times cursed," she whispers. "Three daughters, no sons." She pauses, shoulders hunched, looking to the floor. "I love my daughters, but they cannot carry on the work when Simon is too old. You've no idea how Simon frets about it. It is the curse of the Roses, he says, to wait in vain for a son."

"And yet he came to his father and mother."

"Late he came," she murmurs, "late and in extraordinary circumstances." She turns to face me suddenly. I have no idea what she can mean, so I wait for her to continue. "If we do not have a son," she says, "there will be no one to take over. We'll have to sell our boats for labour. We'll lose our property and our standing."

"Your girls can marry," I suggest before I can stop myself. Is it David's desperate passion that prompts my words? "Their husbands can be heirs along with your daughters."

Elizabeth stares at me for a moment. Old as I am, my face burns.

"They must marry men of property. My husband is clear about that," she says. "If not, the business will fritter away to nothing in a few generations." She pauses. "We supply a grateful merchant in Bristol and my husband has written to him of our daughters."

"He has sons, your merchant?"

"Five. Four as yet unmarried. My husband is hopeful. I am

not. Every man values his daughters as prizes. Women know more of the world. We have had to make do ourselves."

I look to the floor for a moment. I have been called so many names signalling moral decay—hag, witch, old devil—but when my husband was alive, I honoured him. I was not making do. I am unsettled by this respectable woman's cynicism and unsure what kind of help she is asking.

"I cannot prepare a love philtre to work between here and Bristol," I say after a pause. "The distance is too great."

"I am not thinking of husbands for my daughters now," she replies. "I'm thinking of a son for myself. I am with child."

She holds her palm to her belly and gives me a twitchy smile.

"Simon doesn't know it yet. No one does. When I tell him he will pace the floor night and day. He will gaze at my bulging stomach wondering, hoping. The house will cease to sleep and the very walls will tingle with worry and anticipation."

"What do you need from me?" I ask.

She springs forward and grabs my hand. "You must ensure it is a boy," she says. Before I can pull back, she has drawn my palm into her stomach. I can feel a small swelling.

"Can you tell?" she asks, her eyes bulging with worry. "Can you tell the sex?"

"It's sex isn't decided yet," I tell her. "I can make a draft to bring out the man in your unformed child. Please."

I pull away and motion her towards my bed. She backs away and sits patiently while I move over to the medicine jars upon my shelves. I feel her expectation tickling my ears like moths' wings. I reach up to the top shelf and lay my fingers on a jar perched on the edge.

———————

A mist rises from the forest floor, though it hardly rained last night. Everything drips—the mushrooms, the rough bark, and the little twigs that catch me as I pass. New buds open like yellowy-green lips parting, yearning for the kiss of the sun. It is the season of universal growth. Birds fly from tree to tree sensing the changes around them and the under-life of the woods scurries about my feet.

I am afraid my physic will not work with Elizabeth Rose. Her need is too great, as is her trust in me. I steeped the goat's testicle in water and made her drink the fluid. This is the accepted cure, yet I feel her curse may be stronger. And if it proves so, if a baby girl emerges from between her legs, I will be denounced as a charlatan by the most important family in the settlement and one of the most influential in the whole Bristol plantation. And if the boy David gets his wish and Sara swoons for him, Elizabeth Rose and her husband will have double reason for choler. So I am here, in the place I feel safest, the place that once promised me eternal welcome. I repeat to myself the words the man of the forest whispered to me: *While the woods embrace you, no spirit or beast can harm you, no strangers or neighbours smite you, no dank ague infect you. When death lies all around you, the leaves and boughs protect you.*

Why do the people of this place always settle by the coast? Are they too foolish to turn around and see what's behind them? The forest is warmer and carries fewer dangers. And life abounds here. Mushrooms grow in a single night, moths and flies appear and attract birds which can feed us. In a few months there will be berries too, and nature will bask in plenty. But the planters here have forgotten how to live on the land, if they ever knew. They have come here on the sea to fish upon the sea. Once settled, they look out to the ocean and turn their backs on nature's stores.

One day they will make maps of this place as they do in England and Ireland. The settlements will show like spiders couching along the ragged coastline while the interior remains a naked, unexplored blank. When I am ill and ready to die, I shall go down to the water where I have no protection. The forest cannot harm me, this I know too well. It eases every sorrow and soothes every pain. When I have had enough of it all, I will turn my back on this protection. I will expose myself to the wretched, heaving ocean. I will let its waves enfold me and pull me to its icy heart. People here have it wrong. The ocean is for the dying, not for the living.

The ocean robbed me of my family when I was still in my prime. My husband, Gilbert, and two fine children, Katherine and John, slain before my eyes, the beach rocks lapping their precious blood. I've hated beach rocks ever since. I can see the sun's glint in their greedy, wet eyes after the tide pulls away.

My younger two, Mark and Mary, were captured by the pirates. I remember how Mary's infant fingers clawed the air as she was carried away. The rogues' ship sailed to the rim of the world while I collapsed on the beach, staring and helpless, the tug in my chest growing stronger and stronger. Katherine's newborn baby, Matthew—my first and only grandchild—disappeared. I did not see the infant taken and searched for him for days—in the forest, along the empty beach, under the woodpile—calling a name his young ears would not even recognize as his own. Matthew was my last hope. I had seen him neither slain nor taken. If I could find his helpless form still living, I thought, it would redeem every sorrow I had ever felt. I could teach him about his parents, his grandfather, his uncles, and aunts. It would bring comfort to an ocean of pain and turn ashes to love.

But the pirates had been thorough. Even our fishing boats were set adrift, and for malice, not for gain. Days later one returned in pieces to the cove, its fire-scorched boards bobbing against the tide. I recognized the debris as the remains of our boat from a piece of charred cloth tied to an oar fastening.

Everyone was dead or taken away. When at last I gave up on Matthew, I wandered our settlement alone. I buried the lifeless, fly-blown bodies and wept over them. For days I stayed alone. Shadows danced over my shoulder, then disappeared as I turned to greet them. Footsteps scrunched through the shingle and voices called in the breaking waves. I ate in misery, feeling solitude like icy fingers about my neck. Then, as autumn turned to winter, I realized I must leave this strange purgatory. Like a fury emerging from its daze and for the first time noticing the hell that surrounds it, I became suddenly frantic, scambling over rocks, brush, and hill until I arrived, bleeding and delirious, to this cove. John Rose, Simon's father, helped me build a cabin away from the sea and half-removed from the settlement. Rose was a Bible man with tired eyes, hollow cheeks, and a haunted look about his sloping shoulders. He seemed much older than his forty years. With quiet acceptance, he provided for me as he could, leaving food and firewood by my door. We seldom spoke and I was never invited into his home. Whenever I saw him leave a bundle, I would open my door to thank him. He would look up as though he had been spied committing some crime. He would give only the slightest nod before hurrying back to the settlement, to his wife and new baby. Was I a pox, I wondered, to be placated with gifts and sacrifices?

Without question, something kept me apart. It wasn't me. Neither was it the people from the settlement. It was the terrible thing that had happened to me. Grief and misfortune were great walls through which all words sounded garbled like conversations in a dream. I had been reclaimed from hell, but there was a ring of fire around me still, a ring that would scorch the fingers of any who dared approach. It would have burned my own hands, too, if I had tried to reach beyond the horror of my memory. I might be pitied from afar, but I could not be touched.

All I am—this strange old woman living apart, despised yet tolerated, feared yet sought out for my special knowledge—I am because of the pirates. They left me alive but sealed from life.

———

A twig breaks somewhere behind me. I'm slow to turn these days, especially in the forest. And I know there's no need. Few beasts exist to threaten me even if I were not protected. Bears are timid and rare. There are no wild dogs, and I know the sound of wolves; they approach gently, their footfalls like rain, their fur like a breeze brushing the undergrowth.

Lowering myself onto a tree stump, I listen. I hear breathing behind me and sense someone's gaze on my shoulders. The breaths quieten to avoid detection. There is a clumsiness about the presence that can only be human; animals have more grace and are less aware of themselves.

"Come forward and show yourself," I say.

Nothing happens for a moment. I sit quietly and wait.

At last footsteps crunch closer. A shadow cools my shoulders and the figure passes into the clearing in front of me. I look up and it's no surprise to see David Butt, his face quivering and anxious.

"Are you following me, boy?"

He shakes his head distractedly before speaking.

"I have to see what you're doing."

He looks around at the wet twigs, the swaying ferns and grasses.

"I know Elizabeth Rose came to see you this morning. I know she wants you to make a charm so that someone rich will fall in love with Sara."

I stare at the youth's face for a moment. He bites his lip and searches my eyes as though for confirmation.

"How could you make such a guess, boy? Have you been listening at doors?"

His tongue wets his lips. He frowns, despairing. "Then it's true!"

"No, boy, it's false. First, though, tell me how you know Elizabeth came to see me. Were you spying?"

"I didn't need to," he says, throwing up his hands and pacing a semicircle around me. "Sara told me."

"Sara? I thought she never spoke to you."

"She didn't before this morning," he says wincing. He circles in the other direction, glancing at me like a wounded dog. "This morning I was sitting on the wharf skimming stones on the water. I cursed myself for going to you. Foolish cures and potions! The sun mocked my fancy as it always does. Then . . ." The boy circles faster, biting his lip. A curious smile comes to his face. "Then it happened."

"What happened?" I ask. I'm getting dizzy just watching his mad pacing.

"I didn't see it coming. I was lost in my thoughts. The planks creaked beside me. That was the first I knew." He stops, stares at the tree trunk before him, and takes a deep breath. "I turned, and there was Sara. Her shoulder was touching mine. I could feel its warmth through my coat." He presses his hand to his opposite shoulder, reliving the moment. "She picked one of the pebbles from my open palm," he whispers mimicking the action. "She skimmed it across the surface of the water, then . . . smiled at me." He is still talking in hushed tones, as though imparting the whereabouts of secret treasure. "She asked me why I was not fishing with Uncle. I told her about my hand, how I had burned it . . . helping you light a fire. She touched my burn with her fingertips." He stops and looks up to the treetops like a man in torment. "Never, never did I think I would see such a smile from her."

He emerges from this strange ecstasy and becomes agitated again, clutching one hand in the other and padding around in a circle, like a beast of the forest preparing its bed.

I can't help smiling.

"So the charm worked," I say. "What are you worried about?"

"You!" he blasts, suddenly accusing. "I can't believe this happiness is in hands such as yours!"

"Hands such as mine," I repeat calmly.

He shakes his head like a dog tormented by flies. Then he takes a step towards me and holds out his palms in a helpless gesture.

"What can you know of love? What can you know of its torment and its bliss?"

His eyes burn with desperation and his brow furrows with a century of trouble.

"When did I become a senseless rock, boy? When did I cease to have blood, skin, and hair?"

"I mean," he backs away, "I mean it's just too important to leave it to chance. I must be certain."

"Certain of what?" I ask.

He looks towards me again. From the scowl on his face you would swear I had poured a jug of vinegar down his innocent throat.

"Certain you are working for me in this," he says quietly. "Sara told me she knows her mother went to see you. She told me her parents were trying to get a husband for her from Bristol, and that her mother believed you had powers to make sure of it."

I smile and rise slowly from the stump, brushing myself off. "Help me collect some more firewood."

"Tell me it isn't true," he says.

"I've already told you," I assure him calmly. "There are codes for my profession, even in a place like this. I cannot tell you what Elizabeth Rose came to see me about." I stare at him hard. "If I am successful, though," I continue, smiling again, "the result could easily remove the last impediment to a union between Sara and you."

I let the thought sit with him. Breathing the pine of the forest slowly into my lungs, I turn and trudge on towards my cabin. David follows behind, breaking up sticks and branches.

CHAPTER FOUR

What can I know of love? Am I not a worn-out husk, dried out and splintering through years of sterility? Have I not lived apart from humanity so long that I am turned scaly and cold-blooded? Do I not hiss like the snake and breathe sulphur like the dragon?

It's true I live apart from others. And it's true I have played but little role in the lives of this settlement since coming here. I have been a sleepwalker and the people around me are like phantoms. I have outlived horrors that should have incinerated the whole world. And in daring to survive I am given the role most feared by my kind. I have become the hag whose face and form leer from carved doors and gateways in Ireland. I am Sheila Na Gig, the most feared of gargoyles, the vilest of women.

Yet human I am. And tenderness and beauty—the ghosts of those things—are preserved in my heart's core. I am a jar of aspic within which resides the unblemished memory of a love as fresh as spring. Thomas Ridley with his red lips, his coarse, sandy hair, his watery blue eyes. Thomas Ridley and his way of just staring, neither hostile nor inviting, but a rare and graceful beast of the woods, newly emerged into sunlight.

Why should his memory remain after so many years? Why should it be he to whom my daydreams reach? I have married, been widowed, bereaved, and imprisoned. I have been close to starvation, closer to ostracism. I have had connubial bliss. I have given birth to, mothered, and lost children. All without thought of Thomas Ridley. Or so I believed.

But all loves lead back to the first. Thomas Ridley was the essence from which other loves sprouted. He was the clay of my affections. For whomever love was moulded—husband, child, or friend—there was somewhere a hint of Thomas Ridley. Whenever I closed my eyes at night, my husband's hair would lighten to sand and his eyes would wash from brown to blue. Whenever I watched him pull his boat onto the sand, his neck sinews bulging, I would smile, part of me recalling a younger man straining as he unbridled his horse. All men's rituals were an echo of that long-ago morning. And all men were the children of my Thomas.

————

We exchanged not a word in our first three weeks of acquaintance. They moved in briefly, father and son. I watched Thomas Ridley riding circles from my bedroom window. From high in a tree I watched him tramp through the forest beating his stick against the bark. Inside, I watched him eat an apple with a knife, a mysterious and exotic procedure, each angled cut reducing the fruit, his red lips swelling as he bit into the flesh, his pale eyes staring at me through the half light. We were together like this in the pantry, still not speaking, when the front door slammed shut and a voice boomed. I gasped and Thomas did too.

My uncle had returned to find things much altered. There was a commotion, but it didn't last long. Thomas Ridley and I hardly moved until the door slammed once more. The house was silent and we both knew that whatever had occurred was over now. Thomas turned towards me and our gazes locked. Slowly he took another slice of apple and put it thoughtfully into his mouth. We still hadn't exchanged a word, but something had altered. I had seen his fear and he had seen mine. We were no longer strangers.

He made another cut, stabbed the piece with his knife point, and lifted it towards me. I was as overcome as I would have been had I witnessed a statue come to life. My face burned and I found myself giggling. How foolish he must think me, I told myself. Yet he continued to hold his gift until I squirmed and shook my head. Finally, he smiled at me and took the apple piece himself. Alone in my room that night, I went over the scene again and again, trying to imagine myself as he saw me, willing memory to make me more sensible and poised.

Two days later, Mr. Ridley married my mother. Then we were packing boxes and barrels for a journey to England. "Peter doesn't want us to live here anymore," my mother explained to me. "He says we're in more danger because we're Irish. The rebels will take their revenge on us if they break through into the Pale."

I loved this home and did not want to leave. "Mr. Ridley can protect us," I said.

I said this because it was something my mother would be glad to hear. In fact, not only did I not value Mr. Ridley's protection, it was quite an effort to even speak his name. I couldn't help scowling whenever he was near and never spoke in his presence—facts that my mother had noticed and tried, after her own distracted fashion, to correct. So now my words made her soften towards me as I knew they would.

"He would like to, Sheila," she said touching my cheek. "But he spends most of his time in London and we must follow."

My mother flitted into the next room, pointing out articles for the servants to pack. My gaze was drawn through the open front door. Outside, Thomas Ridley threw a stick for one of his father's hunting dogs. The dog bounded across the gravel, jumped in the air to catch, and then raced back, its golden fur rippling, its tail flapping wildly. I hated leaving, but my idea of home was changing already. The lanky boy shaking the dog's ears and whispering encouragement was an integral part of that change. He turned towards me, smiled, and raised the stick for another throw. When he leaves this house for England with his father, I thought, he will be ripping the warm hearth from its structure and taking it with him. It was true that the man of the forest was my friend, and that I gained daily comfort among his leaves and branches. But he was to be found anywhere there were trees, and I would discover him again no matter where we lived.

I watched Thomas Ridley hurl the stick. The big animal bounded after, tongue hanging sideways from his mouth. I smiled at the dog. We had much in common, I thought.

———

It was on the road from Bristol to London that he first spoke to me. Our carriage was part of a caravan rumbling east. Our possessions, our servants, and Mr. Ridley's household made fourteen carriages in all. Mother and Mr. Ridley were somewhere up ahead. Thomas Ridley and I were near the rear of the procession. For the first hour of the journey we sat side by side without any sign of recognition. Both of us watched the barrels and boxes piled up on the opposite seat creaking and bumping together with each jolt of the road. I could tell his posture—hands folded on his lap, head slightly to one side—and I could even hear his breathing beyond the noise of the road.

From Dublin to Bristol had taken four days. I had scarcely seen him on the ship and had given up on his company, at least until we reached London. I was not prepared when at the start of the journey from Bristol he opened my carriage door, especially as I had heard Mr. Ridley bellowing instructions that he ride with the groundsmen. I assumed he had made a mistake and would correct himself the moment he saw me. Instead, he hauled himself up and, to make room for himself, picked up the box beside me and added it to the top of the pile opposite. He glanced at me as he sat down and quickly looked away again. I thought I saw a faint blush on his neck, but the light in the carriage was too weak to be sure.

When I got used to him sitting beside me, I took my gaze from the boxes and barrels in front of me and stared out of the window. Sunlight flickered blindingly, blocked then released by overhanging branches. The world was a patchwork of colour and darkness, I thought. My father was slain one day. I fell in love the next. One moment there were robbers, demons, murderers crouching by the highway, the next the sunlight kissed my face and lit up the greenery of the forest like a celebration of midsummer. Wild roses bobbed in the breeze, their petals as red as the lips of Thomas Ridley. Mosquitoes spun in delirium, insane with happiness.

I groaned in pleasure as the sun held its own for a spell. Its heat mingled with the passing breeze caressing my hair and warming my forehead. I had never been drunk but imagined this was how it felt.

Without thinking, I turned back to the interior of the carriage to stare at Thomas. There was nothing there at first, only multi-coloured suns and darkness. As soon as I could see his outline, however, I spoke. "Are you looking forward to London, Thomas?"

There was silence for a second. The sun flashed on his face and I could see he was amazed, his pale-blue eyes wider and more alive than I had seen them before.

"You speak English!" he exclaimed.

I took my fingers from the window ledge and turned completely towards him now.

"Of course I speak English!" I said. I found myself laughing like a river suddenly bursting its banks. "What ever made you think I didn't?"

"My father," he said, his voice gentle. "He told me I shouldn't try to talk to you because you wouldn't understand."

He continued to stare at me, but his pale-blue eyes were moist and smiling now. "All this time we could have been talking together!" he said with a laugh.

I felt warmed by his attention but suddenly shy about myself. Had I really not spoken a word in his presence? What a strange creature I must seem to him now! And there was something else rather disquieting in all this. However silent I had been, surely Mr. Ridley must have known I understood and spoke English. He knew the history of our family, that my first years were spent in this country before we were offered land in the Pale. He knew that, despite their Irish birth, both my parents used the English tongue. How could Mr. Ridley really have believed I knew only Irish? Unless, of course, he was deliberately misleading his son.

"Well, it doesn't matter now," said Thomas Ridley, perhaps noticing my frown. "I'm delighted you speak English and I'm glad we can get to know each other better before you go away again."

The words took a moment to seep into my head. *Away again.* The echo came once, twice, three times. "What do you mean before I go away again?"

Thomas Ridley shifted in his seat and frowned.

"You haven't spoken to your mother?" he asked.

"About what?"

"There is a convent school in France, Sheila. I think they mean to send you."

"She hasn't said anything to me!"

I must have shouted this rather than spoken it, because Thomas Ridley looked distressed and held out his hands as though to calm me. "Perhaps I have the whole thing wrong," he said. "My father only mentioned it yesterday, and only then because I asked about you."

I sat in silence listening to the grinding wheels. The patchwork world had plunged me into darkness again, it seemed. "How could any respectable English woman be educated in Catholic France?" I broke out suddenly. "No one would receive me."

"No," said Thomas Ridley doubtfully, his brow furrowed. "I must have got it wrong."

I watched the shade of branches skimming across his troubled face and thought of my mother, how she flitted like a shadow from room to room as she prepared for the journey. I recalled a sickly smile directed at me once or twice; it had been like catching a reflection in a window. I was never quite sure if the look was meant for me or if she even remembered my presence for longer than a person waking from a sleep remembers the details of a dream. Could I rely on her?

"My mother would never send me away, especially without talking to me first," I said with a conviction which took even me by surprise. Thomas looked at me with his pale eyes. There was a new kind of respect in his expression. The words, I realized, made me feel better. I was staking my land, proclaiming to the world that I will be moved no further. I was so certain of the justice and good sense of this stance, I became certain, too, that I had power to ensure its accomplishment.

Sunlight flickered into the carriage again, skimming Thomas's hair like flame. "That's wonderful," Thomas said, his smile bright and genuine. "Then I was mistaken."

I don't know what I was expecting from Thomas Ridley, but it wasn't this. I had spent so much time watching him play with his dog and groom his horses that when I longed for his attention I imagined him teasing me, pulling my hair, or tumbling me along the ground while he laughed. I had basked in a hundred pleasing daydreams of this kind. So his polite and solicitous behaviour was a surprise, and one that held some disappointment. He had set me quite apart from his more rambunctious side and I felt there was a barrier between us. I longed to scuffle, to prod his muscles, and tousle his sandy hair, but instead I had to hold back, smile, and answer demurely.

As my disappointment abated, however, I began to see a profound flattery in his manner. And it made me feel older than I had ever felt before. At thirteen I was not a girl anymore. But I had never until now seen myself as a woman. In Thomas Ridley's pale eyes and polite smile I witnessed a reflection of the creature I would become. My mother, I had noticed, drew the finest manners even from the most boorish of men—Mr. Ridley for instance. Thomas was not like his father. And it was exhilarating to think that, of all men, it was gentle Thomas who should be first to reserve the best side of himself for me. These were the types of attentions, I realized—not the boisterous, physical ones—that ladies were gratified to receive. I had entered into womanhood at exactly the same moment I had entered into love. Suddenly the world was a vast, enchanted garden.

We rolled through the countryside for many hours, coming to a stop at an inn some forty miles from London. The journey would take two days, we had been told, so by the end of the next day we would reach London. Thomas Ridley opened the door and jumped down, holding out his hand to take mine. I stepped from the coach, returning his smile. The sunset burned between the trees and the dark inn swamped us in shadow. Every moment now confirmed the start of something new. Even the air had taken on a different scent, mingling hints of evening blossoms and wine. I found my steps slower, my back more upright. I still longed to jump on Thomas Ridley's back and scuffle him to the ground, but the urge was giving way to something more delicate, something requiring stillness and silence.

"Thomas!" came a call from far ahead in the coach procession. I recognized Mr. Ridley's voice.

Thomas immediately took off, running over the crusted earth and gravel. He wove between coaches, disappearing from my sight.

"Just helping the young lady down, Father," I heard him say breathlessly.

"I told you not to bother about that," came the gruff reply. "Go with the boy here and see our horses are treated well."

A chill came into the air. I pulled my coat more tightly around my shoulders.

CHAPTER FIVE

L ondon is a sewer, but I long for it now. In London, I was accused. In London, I was imprisoned. In London, I smelled the stench of purgatory from the cells below and I heard the wailing from that dark place. At night I thought that sound might extract my spirit. I thought it might circumvent death entirely and deliver me straight into the fiery belly of hell. London meant all these things to me, but if I could leave this desolate, friendless place and go back there now, I would think seriously about it.

I wasn't old then, of course, and age, it seems, is the worst of all crimes. Perhaps the people here spurn me because I remind them of what they will become. I am the skeleton swinging from the gibbet. *Commit the crime of living too long*, the wind sings through my bones, *and this will be your fate*.

Is this why these people hide and crouch from the world when they come to the door? Is this why I receive so little open

thanks when I help them? The boy David Butt brings me firewood, and Elizabeth Rose will beg her husband for partridge in
the fall so she may bring it to "the crone." Of course, she won't
mention the source of her debt. She will call it charity, and the
people down below will brim with pride that such generosity
lives among them.

I miss London because it levelled all people to dirt. This
whispering settlement targets only me. Something smarts inside
my brain at this. Why should I be reduced to dispensing cures to
people who despise me? Why should I accept their grudging
favours in return? Surely this is not my intended fate. This must
be some accident, some fault in the great design which went
unrepaired. Where are the children and grandchildren who
should be looking after me? How came their blood to be spilled
onto the senseless, useless rocks? Generations of my family ven-
erated their old people. They were as respected as pharaohs. But
here I am, staring at the smouldering log which gives barely
enough heat. Even for this small comfort I had to humour a child
who distrusts me.

And things grow worse. For the second night running, the June
air has turned icy with the falling of night. I don't know how I can
survive another fall and winter. Listening to the crackling of the
fire, I close my eyes and try willing myself into a happier time. I
hardly notice the knock at the door. It must be close to midnight.
The people of this settlement never come to me this late. No doubt
they imagine demons and serpents guarding my door at night while
dark revelries take place within.

The knock comes again and I open my eyes. Pulling the blanket tighter around my shoulders, I push myself up from the chair.

It's not timid enough for David. Surely Elizabeth wouldn't have returned at this hour. I shuffle across the boards and pull the door open to find the dark outline of Sara Rose.

She isn't shuffling her feet like David, nor is she cowering and glancing down to the settlement like her mother. She is perfectly still; her moulded shoulders are like the branches of a proud young tree, her slim waist clearly defined above her hips like a woman, not a girl. Without asking, she picks up her skirts and walks around me into the cabin. I turn around and close the door. She stands looking at the fire. I start shuffling back to my chair, but she beats me to it, lowering herself into my cabin's only real seat with the confidence of a great lady. She gazes at the fire.

"Are you going to deny it?"

It is more of a statement than a question.

I make my way slowly to my bed and lower myself onto the straw mattress. She doesn't take her eyes from the fire.

"Deny what, child?"

"I'm not a child." Now she turns to me, her eyes moist and resentful. She *is* pretty. David Butt is right about that. Her full cheeks show red, even in the muted glow of a dying fire. Her hair is golden. Her eyes are large and greenish-hazel, and her lips, when they are not pouting, must be generous and shapely. I believe I looked a little like this myself once. In appearance she is the fair maiden of legend. But what pride and what presumption!

"I am eighty years old, Sara. You are thirteen. To me that makes you a child."

She makes a disdainful hissing sound and looks back towards the fire.

"You're trouble. You're an outcast. I've been warned about you a thousand times."

If I were not tired and old, I would get up and box her ears. As it is, my anger dies almost as quickly as it flares. I am left in some bleak limbo of acceptance.

"Who warned you about me?" I ask wearily.

"Father, Grandfather before he died, Mother . . . everyone."

"Your mother!" I laugh.

She glares at me.

"What did you come here for, Sara?"

My voice is steady and I meet her stare. She casts her gaze back to the fire.

"You must undo whatever you have done to me."

"And what is that?"

"I know David Butt comes here. We followed him, my sister Emma and I. We waited in the woods behind your shack until he left." Her fingertips push away a strand of hair that has fallen over her cheek. She looks deeper into the flames. "Emma believes he is in love with me. We know what you did. You cast a spell to make me feel the same about him."

"How could you know this?"

She turns and glares at me again.

"I'll tell you how. Next day, I saw him on the wharf and something came over me. I couldn't help flirting with him. It was just in fun, at first. But when I felt his rough hands with my fingers, something changed."

"People feel what they feel, child. You had never been near enough to him to notice before."

Her eyes narrow. "How could I feel such a thing for David

Butt? He has no property, no boats of his own. He has no parents, even—"

"His father was killed in a storm, Sara," I interrupt. "His mother died of fever."

"I will not fall in love for charity!"

Sara gets up from the chair and faces me. "My family are the leaders of this community. We always were. I and my sisters will marry suitable men, men of property and standing."

"Then you will go far afield, young woman," I say, "for I see none about here who can be described thus."

"You're right," she says, her shoulders straightening. "The Roses are the only family of standing in this settlement. My father is in contact with a family in Bristol."

"So, why are you here?"

"Tell me why David Butt came to see you."

She stands over me now, her eyes keen yet somehow a little frightened.

"I never reveal the purpose of a visit," I reply with what I hope is enough defiance to deter her. She watches me carefully, trying to sift clues from my voice. I decide to distract her with a challenge. "If you have feelings for David Butt, it is because you have feelings for David Butt. Since you're so proud of your bloodline, why don't you draw upon your natural nobility and fight these inappropriate desires in yourself? Here's a chance to prove yourself, girl. The higher the rank, the more control you must exert over your feelings."

It seems I have struck the right note. Her body relaxes a little and she glances around the cabin as though waking from a daydream. "Of course I have the strength to fight these feelings. I'm not in love with David Butt and I'm not afraid of you."

She turns quickly and walks to the exit. She opens the door and turns back to me. "If I find you have been practising witchcraft," she says, "I'll tell my father."

Before I have a chance to reply, she strides into the night, leaving the door open behind her.

————

I haven't slept much tonight. It's colder than any grave in my cabin and a strange paralysis has gripped my heart, preventing me from rising and throwing more logs on the fire. These are not really my logs, a stubborn voice tells me. I did not gather them myself, nor did my kin. These logs are a favour squeezed out of an unwilling boy. My body refuses to move and make use of them.

Perhaps it is the overweening young Sara Rose who has reawakened my own pride. Whatever the cause, I am like a sick animal refusing food, rejecting the state in which I find myself. Warmth and food will keep my heart beating, but they are no longer my friends. They make me survive merely to suffer indignities. I want to reject all sustenance that stops short of restoring me to the woman I should be: a proud, brave, well-loved soul who died in spirit when her family was stolen or slain. How could such a woman scrape for favours the way I do? How could such a woman have lived so long beyond her time?

Yet live I did. Not only did I live on, but I lived on in health and fitness, with appetites and wants. My wits did not scatter to the winds. I did not withdraw into a sweet cave of madness where I might see my family about me still.

I used to think there was a reason I was spared. In the early years, after I first arrived here, I thought the settlement would reclaim me somehow. They might come to me, I thought, and suggest I move my house closer so that I would be in the cove with the rest. I hated the sea, it is true, yet I could have been persuaded. But month after month, year after year, nothing changed. The fear and pity they felt for me hardened into something immovable. They heard I had cures, so they came to me once in a while. But they were usually alone and rarely talked more than they needed. Children never came. One day, four years after my arrival, I looked out of my window to see young Simon on the brow of the hill staring at my cabin. His fingers were in his mouth, and his eyes were round like full moons. I recognized him from the blue wool jacket I had heard one of the women praise. He stood there swaying from side to side like a doll. The sun shone upon the path and the breeze whispered in his blond hair. Was this some emissary, I wondered, sent to recall me to life? Silently as I could, I slipped through the doorway so that I could see the child up close. When I turned the corner of the house and emerged onto the path, I saw he was crouching to the ground, gathering something up in his tiny fingers. I took a step further and he raised himself up again. There was a movement from his infant arm and dust flew into my eyes, pebbles scraping my cheek then scattering around my feet. It was so unexpected, I shut my eyes tight. Phantom suns glared in the darkness and I heard his small feet scurrying down the hill.

"I've been warned about you a thousand times," the girl, Sara, said. The words have me blinking once more as though she, too, had hurled dust in my eyes. "Father, Grandfather . . ." she said. Why would Simon Rose talk evil of me? Had he turned events upside down in his mind? Does he believe he was attacked by the strange woman on the hill? That sunny day almost forty years ago was the only time there has ever been direct contact between us. I've seen him down by the wharf when I've had to go into the settlement. I've seen him on the path and in the forest when he is hunting. But he always looks away. Once I saw him with Sara when she was no more than three winters old. They were together under the canopy of pine, father crouching low, talking softly of the forest to his child. I spied them through a lattice of branches which dripped with melting snow, and felt the magic of their communion. He was drawing the child into the detail, the tattered edges of the cone where the birds had made their meal. In the gentle crow's feet of his smiling eyes I saw a kindness that was familiar to me, and, in the silent wonder of the child, I saw something too. I was in Ireland again, removed from myself and watching. Simon was my father, and I was that child whose eyes searched the boughs for the finches which had disappeared like spirits. So lost in their world was I that I neglected to remain hidden.

"There!" cried young Sara, clapping her hands and turning to her father. Her search for the missing birds had unearthed a different prize and she pointed at me as though she had won a game. I smiled at them both, but Simon's expression had changed already. He picked up his daughter, turned, and made his way from me. "No!" came the cry of the daughter who stared at me open-mouthed from over her father's retreating shoulder.

For years I wondered what harm he thought I meant his young Sara. Had I become so irretrievably tangled up with some infant nightmare of his that he felt he must pass the confusion on to his children? Later, when Elizabeth became ill with Mary and I was warned by the community to stay away from a home I had never been to in the first place, I lost patience. I barred my door and refused to admit anyone for days. I softened after a while as I knew I must and the timid knocks of the sick and anxious found a way into my world again. But what about John Rose? This part of the puzzle is the one that hurts me most. What could charitable, shy John have said against me? Or was the girl merely lying? Feeling around this question like a beetle probing for rot, I find an uncomfortable answer. She was many things, that girl—vicious, arrogant, rude—but it seemed likely that she was telling the truth.

Daylight creeps into my cabin. I shift slowly onto my side. Why should I not march down to the cove and ask Simon Rose why he should talk ill of me to his daughter? I know I will not do this, but it is a stirring thought and pleases me. There are high walls around me and the only freedom I have comes from trust. I never argue, cause trouble, or break a confidence. This is my only safety and I am not quite ready to sacrifice it, even though I lie in the cold.

I shift onto my back and gaze into the milky dawn of my cabin. The straw mattress makes scrunching noises beneath me. I take in the scent of the earth; the sods lying on the roof overhead have come alive again now it is summer. There'll be insects and wriggling things now there is warmth and moisture during the day. I find myself smiling and realize my thoughts have skipped on to Thomas Ridley. The boy had the wholesome smell of the earth and early summer is his season. Perhaps I have given him a passing thought or two every summer since that burning night at the inn between Bristol and London. But this is different. These days he is not far from my thoughts most of the time.

I remember the dark-timbered room of the inn, how the moonlight skimmed along the floor once my candle was out. An oak tree brushed against my window and cast shadows of its leaves all over the walls, so that my room seemed like an arbour of oversized vegetation. A stubborn twig beat a rhythm against the glass and the air was heavy with blossom. I lay awake amidst layers of darkness trying to gauge the changes inside me. I felt like an alchemist's vessel and I could sense my blood altering with the infusions of fate and circumstance. The journey had unsettled me and the summer made me restless. But Thomas Ridley climbing into our coach, treating me like a lady, turning the full attention of his pale blue eyes upon me—these things had pushed me entirely over the edge. I was turning golden inside. I needed the alchemist to return to his experiment and confirm its success.

The building creaked and footsteps drummed along from one quarter of the inn to another. My heart beat faster whenever these footsteps seemed to approach, then slowed again when they moved further off. I couldn't understand my excitement until a footfall, softer than the rest, came very close to my own door. Whoever it was seemed to stand there for a while. There was silence, then a creak, then silence again. Then it came—a soft tapping at my door. My heart rolled like thunder. I sat up.

"Yes?" I said too quietly to be heard, I thought. But the listener's hearing was acute and the door began to open.

And there was Thomas Ridley, still dressed in day breeches and shirt. He looked like a young deer, his pale eyes large, his movements slight but swift. In the wavering light of his candle, he gave an apologetic smile. I think I was smiling too, but I couldn't think of what to do or say. We remained gazing at each other for some moments, he on the threshold with his candle, me sitting in bed cradling a knee in my hand for support.

"Everyone is in bed now," he whispered at last, protecting his candle with his hand. He kept his eyes towards the flame and frowned slightly, shifting on his feet. For a moment I thought he would turn and leave. I still could not think of what to say. I smiled foolishly, trying to form words that wouldn't come.

He sighed, bit his lip, and shrugged. He took a half-step backwards and began to turn, so I quickly cleared my throat and said the first words that came into my head. "Come in and watch the shadows."

He stared at me, questioning.

"Come in," I urged again. He did as I asked and closed the door quietly after him. "The moon is throwing giant shadows over the walls." I turned and pointed to the wall above my bed. But there were no shadows there now because Thomas Ridley's candle had washed them away.

Thomas looked at me, smiled, and came a step or two closer.

"You'll have to blow that out to see them."

I heard his lips part. It was like the first pat of rain before a torrent. He blew out the candle. A dot of fire remained on the wick briefly, then disappeared.

The shadows of the leaves returned, but we had forgotten them already. Somehow and without noise, Thomas Ridley had made his way onto my bed. My hands were running over his shoulders and arms as a fast-moving stream washes over boulders. I pulled his shirt blindly one way and then another to find my way inside. His warm lips touched my cheek and then I felt the weight of his head on my ribs.

Oak leaves hissed against the glass and the lone twig tapped a pendulum rhythm. The shadows bloated as the moon arced high, then rose to the ceiling as the great orb sank. Soon dawn burned pink through the trees and the twig tapped loudly to the strengthening breeze.

CHAPTER SIX

The whole world rumbled, the words *thom-thom-thom-thom* vibrating like a giant drum. Burning lava spewed into the valley, hissing *ridley-ridley-ridley* as it slid down the mountainside. Men, women, and children scattered, screaming *"help-us-thom-as-rid-ley!"* their togas flying, their eyes in panic. Even the chickens cackled *ridley-ridley-ridley*, their flightless wings battering the air. The Forum fell with a great, booming *THOM!* Dust rose and thickened, whispering, *as-ridley-ridley*.

I awoke from Pompeii to find the noise was real enough. Footsteps were thumping somewhere below. "Thomas Ridley!" came a loud, angry voice, not for the first time, it seemed. "Where are you?" It didn't take much time to identify the voice of Thomas's father. It took even less to answer his question.

Thomas Ridley's warm arm lay across my bare belly. His hair pressed into my cheek. I raised my hand and touched his elbow with my fingertips. The day outside was bright and sunny. The oak leaves rustled joyfully against the window. The lone twig prodded the glass as if to say *I warned you.*

My companion breathed in slowly, coming awake.

"Thomas!" the voice boomed again.

Thomas tilted his head a fraction. Wide awake now, he had halted in mid-breath.

"We must wake your daughter, my dear," came Mr. Ridley's voice below. "Our coaches will leave within the hour."

Double footsteps came up the stairs, one set sound and resolute, the other quiet and uneven—a young deer following a wild boar.

Thomas Ridley's pale-blue eyes fixed on mine. His breath touched my face. The tip of his tongue emerged from between his lips and he turned to the door.

The corridor outside vibrated to Mr. Ridley's tread. Already it was too late. Three hard knocks came on the door. I pulled the sheet up to my chin. Thomas Ridley slid under the blankets as far as he could.

"Sheila!" my mother called.

I could not reply.

By the time I heard the door creak open, the sheet was covering my head. I knew they would see both of us right away. How could they not? Thomas Ridley's feet were not covered, neither was one of my arms.

Not a word was spoken. I tried to imagine what they were doing as the floor creaked. Someone—Mr. Ridley, by the boar's tread—came right to the foot of the bed. I expected the blankets to be pulled violently from us, exposing our nakedness. But there was only hush, then the soft creaking of the floor, then a silent withdrawal to the exit. Eventually, the door creaked shut. I heard whispering outside, then louder conversation retreating to the stairs.

I lowered the sheet from my head. Thomas Ridley stared across at me, then closed his eyes and buried his face in the pillow.

———

Fear can defeat a person more surely than a sword, I realize now as I gaze at the calamity that is my life—the withered timbers of my walls, the cracked medicine jars resting on my shelf, the dried worms, my splintered crossbeam.

I could have answered my mother's call and told her I would be down in a short time. Thomas Ridley could have hidden under the bed as soon as he heard his father's voice. Why did we panic and let our silence give ourselves away?

I push myself up from the straw mattress and lower my feet to the cold floor. Another day in this settlement seems too much to endure.

I wish I could crawl back inside the past. I remember pulling the sheet over my head when my mother called my name. If I could go back to that time like a lizard re-entering its long-discarded skin, I could change everything. If I could answer, "Yes, Mother, I am dressing, I'll be down soon," the whole of my life from that moment on would have been quite different.

I find my old chest hammering at the thought. It's as though this were a call to action, as though part of me believes I could change it all now. I'm sorry for the disappointment that must inevitably descend from my brain to my pulsing veins and racing heart. It's true my whole life turned on this single omission. But it's also true that, once the moment was past, absolutely nothing could be done to change it. I am stranded in old age and misery and I can never return.

At least the dream of going back has given me energy to rise. I make my way towards the door and open it wide. The sky is clear-blue with strings of unmoving clouds very high above the earth. The bright sun kisses the grass and the tops of the trees sparkle in the undulating breeze. The world before me would make me feel almost serene were it not for one detail. David Butt is moping beneath a canopy of branches only a few footsteps from my door. His shoulders are sloping and his hands are buried in his breeches. He gives me a mournful stare when he sees me.

"I've brought you firewood," he says with a sullenness that belies the helpful gesture. Close to his feet is a generous pile of broken sticks and branches. He bends and scoops some up in his arms. Turning with his burden, he approaches the cabin jerkily, like a scarecrow learning how to walk. I move inside and out of the way as he makes for the fireplace and lowers the bundle onto the floor.

"Thank you," I say, pulling back my chair and sitting.

He turns to me as he dusts himself down. "I saw her this morning," he announces, his voice strange, almost cracking. His green eyes catch the sunlight from the doorway and their watery paleness reminds me, for a moment, of Thomas Ridley. "She was on the wharf, pacing, staring out at the sunrise."

He sighs, biting his lip, then crouching down by the firewood again, fingers the twigs at his feet. "I watched from the house for a while," he says, picking up a short stick. "I threw on my clothes and followed her out. Things had gone so well recently, I assumed she was sleepless for me as I have been sleepless for her." He breaks the stick in both hands. "But when I came up to her and touched her shoulder, she spun around and slapped me in the face."

"Did she say why?" I ask.

"She called me a filthy little ruffian," he says with a nervous laugh, "and told me I must never lay a hand on her again." He stares at the broken stick. He is breathing hard and shivering. He says nothing for a while.

"So, what happened then?"

He looks up slowly. I notice red rims around his eyes.

"You must help me, Sheila," he says. "You must help me get away from here. You must tell me how to survive in the woods."

There's a sickening thud in my chest.

"Why would you need to do that?" I ask. "What happened, boy?"

"It's Sunday," he says, standing. "No one was up. They might never know."

"Know what?"

"Nothing. Nothing that concerns you."

"You're scaring me, boy."

"I couldn't stop myself," he whispers. "It happened before I knew it." He puts his hand to his forehead and his eyes flash desperately. "It's all your fault!" he exclaims. "It's your responsibility to help me!"

I continue to stare up at him, waiting, hoping for some explanation other than the one I most fear. He turns away suddenly, shaking his head. "She's gone. Sara's gone. One moment she was mocking me, eyes like darts, tongue like an arrow. Then she was choking, my thumbs on her neck, squeezing."

My head goes dizzy. I lift my hand to my temple and groan.

"But it wasn't my fault!" he says with such certainty I almost believe him. "She made me do it! *You* made me do it too, with your spells! What kind of wickedness gives hope where there is none?" He stares at me with frantic eyes, then blinks a few times as though waking from a dream. He begins pacing in a semicircle around the firewood, opening and closing his fists.

"There is no hope for you, boy," I say, watching him. "A murderer can never live in peace. The act will eat away your soul."

He looks at me, startled, and stops pacing. "I'm not a murderer! I'll tell everyone it was your fault."

"How could it be my fault? I'm too old to have strangled Sara Rose."

He begins pacing once more, but in the opposite direction. "If they find the body, I'd say you put me under a spell. If they don't, I'll say you put Sara under a spell that made her wander off into the woods and never return. They'll believe either of those explanations easily enough."

"Why would they believe such nonsense?" I'm genuinely curious, aware that a mystery might be opening to me at last.

"Because they're all terrified of you," he says with eyes narrowed. "And it isn't nonsense. How do I know you didn't plan this whole thing? How do I know you didn't want me to murder Sara?"

I'm suddenly too tired to hear these questions, and tired of watching this young fool pacing and circling. How do they know

I don't cause drought and mist and cold? How do they know I
don't cause the fish to disappear from the bay and the beasts to
run away from the woods? There is no end to such foolishness
and no defence against it either. Why don't these idiots build me
a scaffold, hang a noose about my neck and be done with it?

"What did you do with Sara's body?" I ask feebly to change
the subject.

"I took it out in Uncle Seth's boat and threw it into the bay
beyond the cove. It might wash up around here. It might be
pulled out into the ocean, or wash up somewhere else."

He's pacing more slowly now, calmed by his decision to put
the blame on me. I put my hands on the sides of my chair and
prepare to rise. "Well, if I'm the murderer," I say, "you don't need
my help. Let's go down together and see who they believe." I
begin to stand but he leaps towards me.

"No!" he says, flapping his hands urgently to sit me down.
"No, you must not!"

"But you said there was no danger they would blame you."

"That's only if I can't survive on my own." His fingers tremble over my head. "I don't want to give you away."

"That's very kind of you," I tell him, settling down again.

"I need to know all about the forest. I know you have charms
to protect me."

I shouldn't have helped the boy. Murder is murder.
Concealment is not only wicked, but futile. But I did feel responsible. I should have warned him when he first came to me that

love could not be forced. I knew his passion was unhealthy, but the boy drew me inside his desire. I felt its heat and its compulsion. And now he has committed the worst of all crimes, there is still something about this clumsy, foolish boy I cannot refuse. Once again I am inside his feverish mind, looking out.

I picture him weaving his way under the pine-scented canopy. I wonder if the amulet I gave him helps him sense the forest's pulsing heart. Does he hear the man of the forest in the rustling leaves? Will he harvest the mushrooms I told him about? Will he set rabbit snares when he gets far enough into the interior?

The settlers have been yelling Sara's name for some while, but no one has come up the hill. It is still early and they are not panicking yet. Perhaps they suppose she has skipped along the shore or rounded the rocks to the next cove. Or maybe that she has hidden herself in someone's home as a jape. But when the sun climbs higher and the waves roll and sizzle for hours on end with no sign of her, things will change. Beyond the settlement— the cluster of homes, the ribbon of beach, and a few bald rocks— there is only an endless murmuring ocean and a vast and unexplored forest. Few have troubled to learn the ways of the woods and, for most, including the Rose children, being lost is the same for an hour as for a hundred years.

Already there is tension in one man's voice, and I can sense him listening hard as his call of "Sa-ra-Sa-ra" echoes around the cove, then dies into silence. This must be Simon Rose. He is trying to decide how angry he should be.

"Sara!" he calls sharply this time. Judging from the voice, he has climbed a little way up the hill. What would it take, I wonder, for Simon Rose to knock on my door? How desperate would he have to be? And what would that extraordinary meeting be like? Two people who have lived for forty years in the same small settlement exchanging words for the very first time.

Simon Rose is silent again as he listens for his Sara's reply. I hear his boots scrape against the dry earth as he turns and goes back down to the settlement.

He will have to come again; it's inevitable. And eventually he will have to come to me. His other daughters might already know that Sara came to see me. They definitely know about David's visits—Sara told me that. Soon they will realize that both Sara and David are gone, and they will connect the two. It occurs to me for the first time that I'm in rather an awkward position. I had better start thinking of some answers.

Another call comes from somewhere down in the settlement. This time it's Elizabeth Rose. The quality of her voice is quite different from that of her husband. Simon's call was tense and threatening. Elizabeth's has all the pain of a wounded animal, of a wolf mourning its cub. The grief of it shakes me and makes me feel a turbulent sadness of my own.

I too was taken from my mother at thirteen years old, pulled from her world and her protection. And while I wailed and mourned the loss, I saw but little grief from her. Elizabeth Rose's plaintive cries remind me of the nurturing tones I was denied. Suddenly I am envious of the dead. It puzzles me that, of all tragedies that have befallen me since, it is this one—my own abandonment—that is stirred by the sound of a mother's grief. I have more recently lost my own children, yet that loss seems not nearly so close. It is not the first time I have felt my girlhood days returning more vividly than the ground that lies between. "Old fools are babes again," my playwright acquaintance once grumbled in his misery, the damp walls dripping around him. He was not old himself, and I thought he was being dramatic. But now I see what he meant. These days I feel the girl in me returning.

———————

Some while after we were discovered, when the footsteps had died quite away, Thomas Ridley moved under the sheets. He slipped off the bed, pulled on his breeches, and fumbled with his shirt buttons. He gave me one swift, terrified glance—a hint of apology perhaps in his pale-blue eyes—and was gone.

I journeyed the remainder of the way to London with two of Mr. Ridley's servants, a tall man and a white-faced woman. They were waiting for me as soon as I opened my bedroom door. "We've been sent to escort you the rest of the way," the woman said with dry urgency, taking my arm and hurrying me downstairs and into the carriage. The man and woman remained, one on either side of me, blotting out the daylight from that moment on.

Through the confusion of it all, I was exhilarated still. The scent of Thomas Ridley was in me. Every sensation of the previous night—his nose nuzzling into my neck, the warmth of his legs, the sweat-dampened arch of his neck—was alive, skimming over my imagination just as swallows dip and hover over the surface of a lake. Even while the woman on my right cast her censorious glance upon me, the coach wheels rumbled his name: *Thomas, Thomas, Thomas.*

I expected this punishment. It was inevitable that we would be separated for a day while my mother made up her mind what to do, and part of me dreaded explaining things to her at the journey's end. But I knew these problems were minor. There was a great joy pulsing in me like a rainbow bursting at the seams. When the smell of London's woodsmoke began to permeate the coach, I became excited again. It would not be long before I would see Thomas again, perhaps even at supper.

But when we arrived at Mr. Ridley's house, I was hurried by the two servants up two flights of stairs. Seeing no one but staff in Mr. Ridley's hallway entrance when we passed through, I refrained from calling for my mother lest it annoy her. I was shown into an attic room with a bed in the corner, a large fireplace, a little food and water already prepared on a tray. On a desk were rolled-up charts and papers. As soon as the door was shut, it was promptly locked from the outside. I went to the window.

It was getting dark. A man was lighting lanterns one by one in the alley far below. Workmen drew carts, the wheels scraping against the cobbles. Women passed by shops with baskets on their heads. Some joked and called to one another. I turned my head slightly and listened to the movements within the house. There were many footsteps, none of them very near, some running up, some down or across; furniture was shunted across floors, and there was a regular babble of voices. I attended very closely to these. Sometimes I fancied hearing myself talked about. I strained to distinguish Thomas, his father, or my mother. Sometimes the muted syllables of a man seemed to form words like, "All right, Thomas, go and fetch her to supper," or a woman's soft tones would seem to say, "She's been punished enough. Can I fetch her?" But then something would be added to render my interpretation senseless: ". . . into the drawing room," the man would add, or, ". . . opposite the fireplace," the woman would conclude. The voice I thought I recognized became one I knew I did not.

Gradually the life in the alley slowed, as did the noises from the house. Footfalls pattered quietly somewhere downstairs. I urged them on, longing to hear them climb towards my room, but a door closed softy and then there was silence. No one would come to me tonight, I realized; not Thomas Ridley with his pale-blue eyes, not my mother with her vague, distracted assurances, not even a servant at whom I might at least fire some questions.

Somewhere, far below, a kitchen maid scoured a pan. Lost in anxiety and fatigue, I lay down on the pillow, nestling my head in the soft feathers so I might draw up some comfort from them. My ear vibrated with each heartbeat as though a giant were striding somewhere beyond London's walls, shaking the foundations of the house. I thought of Ireland, of the warm breezes and rippling leaves. I inhaled the smell of imaginary earth and thought of Thomas Ridley and his thick hair, the colour of sand. I thought of the man of the forest and tried to remember precisely how he had appeared to me. All I could recall were the contours of a face showing in the knots and pits in the tree bark, a face that faded and revealed itself in the shifting light and shadow. I could remember how his voice hissed gently like the rustling of leaves as he spoke. I let the words run through me, then repeated them like a prayer. *The forest is yours,* I told myself. *While the woods embrace you, no spirit or beast can harm you, no strangers or neighbours smite you, no dank ague infect you. When death lies all around you, the leaves and boughs protect you.* My eyes became heavy. I was far from the forest now, it was true, but the pacing giant merged in my imagination with the man of the forest. It was he—the green man—pacing outside the city walls, I told myself, and his mission was to protect, not to threaten. Listening to the *thump, thump, thump* of the man in the forest, I gradually drifted into sleep.

———

Next morning I woke to crisp sunshine streaming in through the window and the clamour of a working city in my ears. Sudden yells and shrieks broke through a constant babble of voices like erratic seagulls crying above a constant, murmuring sea. I went to the window to see this pandemonium. The alley was thick with carts and traders in constant milling movement. The voices wafted up, multiplying against the brick-and-timber walls. I could not match words and speakers together. All sound and movement was spasmodic and random: a woman presenting necklaces on hoops to a passing crowd of ladies; a ragged man with a shoulder beam from which hung wooden cages with twitching chicks; a sudden shriek to which no one paid attention. Did one of the humans below make the sound or did the cry emanate from the stones and dust? Certainly no one turned to see who had made it.

The white-faced woman entered with a bowl of water. I turned from the window to find her laying it by my bed. I thought of stopping her to ask her what was going on, but she had left before I could form any words. I washed my face and hands and started drying them on the cloth provided. Before I had quite finished, she entered again.

"Come," she said. "You are to follow me downstairs into a carriage which is waiting."

She was so decided in manner, her dark eyes so fixed, that I took a couple of steps to the door at her command. Then I forced myself to halt. "Where is my mother?" I asked, my lip stiff and, for the moment, not trembling. "I need to see her."

I was expecting a rebuke, but instead the woman looked at me mildly, her eyebrows raised. "She is at the place to which you are bound. We must hurry."

I had no idea where "the place" referred to could be, but I was happy to rush downstairs with the woman now. Everything would be explained, I thought, all the silence and isolation of the last day and night. Perhaps I would join my mother in one of the London parklands. She might rebuke me at first, or she might have forgiven me already. But soon everything would be as normal and we might walk together, taking in the waters and the meadows.

On the ground floor the servants were still shifting furniture after yesterday's arrival. Two of Mr. Ridley's staff were heaving my mother's heavy oak sideboard in through the hallway. Another three were fixing a place on the wall for her grandest mirror. My gaze swooped eagle-like around the hallway, into the dining hall, for a glimpse of Thomas Ridley, but he was nowhere to be seen. Perhaps he was with Mother too.

The white-faced woman led me swiftly outside and into a small coach. We began to move instantly I sat down. We were silent as the carriage rumbled along, its springs creaking and groaning. It turned one way, then another, passed markets reeking of fish and horse droppings, became trapped in a crowd of ragged-looking people, then lurched forward again at great speed. I glimpsed the Thames, blue and glistening in the sunshine. As we turned once more, I saw from a distance the great white walls of the Tower of London, the flag of St. George flying high from the mast. We came into the shadow of trees. Dark, high walls skimmed by the carriage window. We turned sharply one last time and flew through a rugged stone archway and into a courtyard. There we came to a stop. The white-faced woman alighted first; I followed. Looming over all sides of the enclosed courtyard was a lofty, grey-brick building, its walls as high as the trees I had known in the Pale. Something shrank and coiled inside me as the woman tugged me gently by the elbow and bade me follow her through the entranceway. As we hurried along a dim, high-ceilinged hallway, I could hear from somewhere far beneath our echoing footsteps a distant sound of coughing. A thickset man passed us, a circle of large keys hanging from his belt. He ignored us as though we were spirits, quite invisible to him. I glanced over my shoulder as he unlocked an arched doorway and disappeared, closing it after him with a great echoing clunk. We turned a corner into an identical corridor, and at last, the white-faced woman stopped at a narrow door and knocked. I could barely hear a reply, but she pushed open the door and gestured me to go in first.

I remember the room, the smell of wax polish and oak, the creaking of leather chairs. Mother was sitting, pale and round-shouldered, as if she were in mourning again, though I knew no one could have died. Mr Ridley was right there beside her. He murmured some comforting phrase to her while the white-faced servant led me to the end of the long table at which they sat. She placed her bony hands on my shoulders, like a sculptor getting a measure of its stone. I knew the meaning of her touch: I should remain standing in the place she had put me.

I watched my mother intently, waiting for her to glance in my direction so I could fathom her mood. It had been so long since she, or anyone else, had properly acknowledged my presence I was beginning to feel as if I were indeed a ghost. Opposite Mr. Ridley and my mother was a bull-like man with huge shoulders and a round head. Through his sparse white hair, I could see pink bumps and furrows.

"Indeed," he said, continuing a conversation that must have been in progress before I came into the room. "Bedlam is not the place, Mr. Ridley." He had a reedy voice and a nervous smile, neither of which matched his robust figure. "You did well to think of us. It is a disease of morals, not of wits, and without confinement it would, as you correctly imply, spread and infect your household. From all that you say, the dark lands of Ireland with their pagan lures have her firmly under their spell."

I watched the man's forehead as he spoke, curious about the bumps and abrasions of his permanent frown. I thought about the cratered moon I had glimpsed through the inn window and wondered how a similar surface could be beautiful in one place and ugly in another.

"Young girl," he said abruptly, turning towards me. His eyes were as pale as Thomas Ridley's, but there was a coldness about them that chilled me. His nervousness and humility were gone.

"I want you to answer me truthfully. Your mother tells me you used to go outdoors often in Ireland, to the countryside surrounding your home. Tell me precisely where you went."

"The forests," I said. I looked at my mother again, but still could not catch her eye. Mr. Ridley handed her his handkerchief; Mother took it delicately in her fingers. She seemed a strange creature to me at that moment, a butterfly without colour, fragile and timorous yet somehow not graceful.

"Indeed," said the stranger with a knowing sigh, "and what did you do there?"

"I climbed trees and watched the birds and animals."

The man frowned sadly and looked across the table at my mother, whose face was now half-buried in Mr. Ridley's handkerchief.

"And in that time, young lady, did any of the animals speak to you? Did they become your companions?"

"They were my companions, yes, but they did not speak directly to me. They were animals." I looked from face to face, but met only the stranger's eyes. "Why? What's wrong?"

"Just answer the questions I put to you, girl," the man said, fixing me for another while with his stare. "And did you converse with any other being? Any creatures that you did not recognize as animals?"

Suddenly the room became airless and my face started to burn. He was asking what he already knew. It would be dangerous to try to lie.

"The man of the forest," I blurted out. The burning sensation on my face spread to my neck and shoulders, and my knees began to feel weak.

"The man of the forest?" he whispered. "What man?"

"A man of leaves and branches," I replied. "He whispers like the leaves. He comes and goes like the breeze."

The black centres in the stranger's eyes shrank to pinpricks. His shoulders heaved like those of an animal set for slaughter. "This is more serious than I thought," he said. Mother looked up from her handkerchief. Mr. Ridley narrowed his eyes.

"She is conversing with the green man, the pagan spirit of the forest."

"But all this happened in the Pale, Mr. Jarvis," Mother sobbed. "Surely there could be no pagan spirits in a land under the English Crown."

"I wish you were right, Mrs. Ridley, but things are not so simple. You were protected there by armies and the fortresses. You believed perhaps that the dark lands began only beyond the Pale. Being a good and devout lady, dedicated to the faith of your Sovereign, you were safe from the corrupting influence of paganism and witchery. But a girl on the brink of changes would be so much more receptive to heathen forces than you or—pardon me, Mr. Ridley—your late husband would realize."

"You must not blame yourself," said Mr. Ridley leaning toward my mother, laying his hand on hers.

"No, indeed," agreed Mr. Jarvis. "The very air wafted ungodliness into her lungs. No mother, no matter how devout, would have been subtle enough to prevent her daughter's infection."

My mother nodded gratefully at Mr. Jarvis. "May we hope for a cure?" she whispered.

Mr. Ridley frowned and the lines on his forehead became heavier. "This is a serious case indeed, Mrs. Ridley, and, in the usual course of events, punishable by far worse than mere incarceration." There was a grave silence. My mother held the handkerchief from her face and became as still as rock. Mr. Jarvis, seeing this, leaned back slowly and gave her a reassuring smile. "You must remember, my dear lady, that the creature that stands before you now is no longer your daughter. Even though she may look the same, her soul has decayed from the inside out."

Mother sighed and gazed at the table.

"You may, of course, have your personal physician attend her, though I doubt the expense of it will prove worthwhile. It is her soul, not her mind, which is diseased. And Newgate is not an asylum."

"We had thought of sending her abroad to a religious house," Mother said mildly.

Mr. Jarvis gave her a gentle smile. "She is too far advanced, I am afraid. But you need not give up on her if you are not quite ready. She will be lodged in the master's side and may have any treatments or comforts you deem fit."

"Indeed," said my mother. She buried her face in Mr. Ridley's handkerchief once more.

————

I can't recall how long it took me to work out all the implications of the conversation taking place before me. Now, sorting through their words again, it seems obvious from the start. But at the time, the realization came upon me only in a series of jolts, like the involuntary flinch a body makes from a flying stone. Only when the moment is past does a person have the leisure to question whether the missile was an accident randomly gliding in her direction, or whether there was purpose and intent behind its aim. All I know is that, by the time I finally absorbed the entire meaning of the exchange, I was alone in a stone-walled room with no fire, a thin straw mattress, and a barred window. Only then did I realize that, as a consequence of laying with Mr. Ridley's son, I had been sent to prison.

CHAPTER SIX

I'm still haunted by the expression on my mother's face just before she left the room. I remember standing by the table like a swaying reed as she and Mr. Ridley rose. Mr. Ridley went to the door with Mr Jarvis. At first it seemed as though my mother would do the same. But at the last moment she wafted toward me, raising her hands to my face before dropping them to her sides again in a helpless gesture. She tilted her head and gave me a look of such broken-hearted anguish—her eyes wet with tears, her brow a torment of furrows. Next moment, she was turning from me. As her moth-like figure disappeared through the doorway, I heard her greeted by the soft and comforting words of her new husband.

―――――

The settlement has come alive in the search for Sara. For hours now I've been listening to the growing tumult. I've heard footsteps approach to within a few yards, then trudge back down the hill. I've heard Sara's name called frantically from the village, from the shore, and from the woods on the other side of my cabin. Sometimes everything goes quiet for a short time and I'll hear muted voices and whispering. There's something ominous in the fact that no one has yet knocked on my door. It's as though a wolf pack is circling, cutting off possible routes of escape as it closes in.

So much effort for one spoilt girl, the phrase comes to me unbidden. I despise myself for thinking this way, but I cannot help it. I'm jealous of this cruel and pretty creature. Her loss has caused the world to cease, when my incarceration caused hardly a bump.

I could not begin to decipher the sorrow on my mother's face that day in Mr. Jarvis's office. Was it pity for the sufferings I would undergo in jail? I turned this question over and over in my head in the days that followed, as if it were a die with no markings. Always the same question rebounded in place of an answer: Why then would she have put me there?

Other unpalatable solutions emerged, but I found ways to bend my mind to some urgent and distracting task to avoid taking them in. I still do the same, even though I have the answer. The solution is like a monster whose contours were revealed by an unwelcome dawn. It is no less fearful, but I know its shape and the size of its fangs. I know what it is now that I work so hard not to think about. Today, however, the panic for Sara is forcing the issue upon me with unusual persistence. I relive the moment when my mother raised her hands to my face, then dropped them to her sides, tilting her head. I remember how she gazed at me with tear-filled eyes. I cannot deny there was accusation as well as sorrow in her expression, and that the two emotions were entwined as one. I have forced her to abandon me, her wet eyes seem to tell me. It is her predicament, not mine, that grieves her.

There's a knock on my cabin door. My heart hardens like stone.

"Yes?" My response is scarcely audible, even to myself.

The door opens slowly and I rise swiftly from my chair. Like a fox's terror as it flies from the hounds, my fear has given me an ease of movement I have not possessed for some while.

Elizabeth Rose slips in quickly and shuts the door after her.

"Have you heard the news?" she asks, her large eyes startled and blinking.

She's been found, I think. Her body has washed up on the settlement's shore.

My mouth tries to move, but I say nothing.

"It's my Sara. She's gone!"

"Gone," I reply hoarsely. And I marvel at the way the situation has conspired to disguise my guilt. Yes, I'm trembling, but such reaction is in keeping with the intelligence I have just received.

Elizabeth takes another step towards me.

"She's been missing since early this morning. No one knows where she is."

I find myself backing off towards my bed. Elizabeth makes for the chair I have left and sits on its side, facing me. I lower myself onto the straw mattress.

"It's my punishment," she says, gripping one hand in the other. "I know it."

"Punishment for what?" I manage to say.

"I told you I was three times cursed by my daughters," she says and leans forward as though in pain. "I tried to interfere with fate and change the child inside me, and now Sara is stolen away."

My body begins to calm. The woman before me is like one bound in rope. Anxiety and guilt coil around her spirit, and she cannot see beyond them to notice the suspicious behaviour of another.

"I have sinned against nature and against God," she continues, "and this is my punishment."

"But it is not yet dusk," I say, my voice steady. "She will turn up."

"No," she sighs, staring at the floor. "She is gone. I can feel it. Something happened when I tried to interfere with the course fate has laid out for me. And it may be more than that."

She is motionless for some while. I find myself tensing again, wondering if she knows more than she is saying about Sara and David.

"What do you mean?" I ask softly.

"There is a general curse on us," she murmurs. "All of the Roses. Simon's mother also struggled for years to provide an heir. In trying to break the curse now, I have sinned against nature."

"That makes no sense. The curse was already broken with Simon."

She looks up at me slowly.

"Not really," she says. "Simon did not come to his family in the usual way."

"You said that to me last time; I didn't understand it then."

"I can say no more. We never talk about it, and my husband trusts you least of all the people in the settlement."

She does not mean to be cruel, I know, and her voice is without passion of any kind. I find myself drawn to the question again.

"Why does he trust me so little? We have never met."

Elizabeth shakes her head slowly. "Something his father used to tell him, I think. He was warned never to speak to you." She looks up at me again with a wan, sickly smile. "He is still afraid to this day."

The idea is grotesque. A child throwing dust in the eyes of a stranger needs little explanation. A child's mind is full of monsters and shadows. But a man carrying those infant terrors through forty years of life is beyond all reason. And why would John Rose tell his son such a thing? Even though he seemed aloof and distant, he had helped me settle near the community and thought about my needs. Why would he give with one hand and take away with another?

"Tell me true, Sheila," Elizabeth says, her eyes suddenly bright with anxiety. "Did my Sara ever come to see you?"

Suddenly I am bound at the stake. I can feel my scrawny arms pinioned by the question as though it were a restraining leash.

"No, never." The words spill out before any decision is made. I had no choice. Hesitation would defeat me as surely as a bad answer. My ears buzz and I watch her reaction. She looks to the floor again and sighs.

Have I just built my own funeral pyre? Any stray spark might now ignite the ground upon which I stand. If Sara told one of her sisters about last night's visit, if someone saw her enter my cabin, the dry wood beneath me will burst into flame. I will be exposed as a liar and such a lie, with Sara gone, would be lethal.

"What about the boy, David Butt?" she asks while I am still numb from shock. "His Uncle Seth cannot find him today either."

"David?" I say slowly. *Don't lie!* I tell myself. *Don't lie this time! Emma and Mary Rose know he has been seeing you!* "Yes, David comes to see me often. He brings me firewood."

"Sheila, you must tell me, did David ever ask you about my Sara? Did he ever show any interest in potions or love philtres?"

Again I must speak before thinking. "Yes, David was in love with your Sara. He asked me about it often and I played along to humour him." I can't believe I sound so calm while my chest is hammering so hard. "But I do not practice physic on children."

Elizabeth looks at me and nods.

"I don't know how this will end," she mumbles. "Simon is beside himself."

She rises from the chair and turns to the door.

I know I should tell her not to worry, that Sara will turn up, but the words cannot form on my dry lips. I watch her go to the door, knowing I am not cruel enough to give hope I know to be false.

She opens the door and turns to me.

"I know she is gone," she says, her eyes tired and blinking. "A mother knows." She disappears and closes the door after her.

———

The barred window looked out onto a narrow, empty courtyard, not the same one through which the carriage had entered, but a tiny irregular space. There was no entrance or exit; it looked like the bottom of a hastily dug well. My cell was at least one storey from the ground and the window was so small I had to push my forehead close to see anything above, below or on either side of a patch of grey stone wall opposite. Gusts of wind spiralled in the little trough, taking specks of dust and dry straw in a zigzagging ride, then died and let them fall. The heavy door behind me was oak inlaid with iron. When it closed, it made a noise like thunder.

Despite all clear evidence to the contrary, my chest heaved with the urgent belief I could escape. So great was my determination, and so young my spirit, I did not stop to ponder the many differences between reality and desire. I went to the door and banged against it. The wood was so thick it made almost no noise, though my knuckles became raw very quickly. Still, I was undeterred. I went to the window and hauled at one of the iron bars in an attempt to dislodge its base from the stone. I gritted my teeth and strained my sinews, but nothing at all happened. I felt like a flea trying to shift the walls of a cathedral.

I was still certain that there were a hundred opportunities for escape yet to make themselves obvious to me. Like an acrobat warming up for a performance, my mind was working through these possibilities, when a heavy *clunk* came from the door. I backed away to the bed as it began to open. In came a plump, pale-faced woman with a grimy white cloth wrapped many times around her head. She carried a tray and smiled at me as she placed it on a low table by the bed. I was amazed that she had left the door open behind her and thought this must be an oversight. But a tall jailor with a dirt-encrusted face stood in the corridor watching me with blank and unperturbed eyes. At first glance I thought that, like the woman, he was old. Decay and age hung around everything. But beyond the grime his face seemed unwrinkled; he was perhaps no more than twenty. A ring with a set of keys hung from his belt.

"You're the new girl, aren't you?" the woman said in a not unfriendly manner. She rubbed her hands together and looked down at the tray. "There's bread, mutton scraps, milk, and water. It's not so bad. You'll be well looked after here." The guard in the corridor sniffed, but his expression didn't change. "This is the best part of Newgate," the woman continued, "the master's side, and your people have left an allowance for your food and comfort." She pulled a joint-stool close to the low table and beckoned for me to approach.

I could see she was trying to bestow comfort, but there was an alien whiff about her that was intolerable. It carried hints of brick dust, rotten food, and human waste long dried to powder. The same curious smell wafted in from the corridor and the sallow-faced young guard. This stench seemed the very essence of captivity; my pulse raced in opposition to it. I resented the woman's attempts to be pleasant. I did not intend to stay, and the idea that I might need her reassurances was repulsive to me.

The woman smiled again, preparing to leave. Suddenly I could bear it no longer. The door was open and I was destined to go through it as surely as a ferret is destined for a rabbit hole. I made no decision but simply took flight, dodging past the woman and leaping through the open doorway while ducking under the guard's arm. The corridor gained in a single shimmy, I bounded through its narrow walls towards one end where crisp beams of sunlight seemed to promise an opening.

"Gilbert! Quick!" I heard the woman shout.

The guard's heavy footfalls were close behind, so I didn't dare to slow down, even though one of my sandal straps broke, the whole shoe flying away from my sole and flapping against my ankle with each bound. The light ahead of me that had promised escape revealed itself now as merely a barred window gaping into the sun. I swayed one way, then another, in case the guard made a grab, then scambled around the corner from this false mirage, pushing myself off against the stone wall.

I chased down a corridor much narrower than the one through which I had just run. The guard shouted something I didn't catch, but there was desperation in his voice. I felt that either I must be leaving him behind or I must be coming very close to an egress through which I could make my escape. Taking another corner, I jolted to a stop. This was another long corridor along which stood three guards some twenty yards apart, each with his back to an archway. These must be either cells or new passageways, I thought. Or perhaps one was an exit to the street. If I knew which one led to freedom, I felt sure I could wrestle any guard to the ground. My heart thumped with the ferocity of a young lioness and my fists clenched with the bare-knuckled fury of the cruelest barbarian living beyond the Pale. The nearest of the guards turned to me with mild amusement and smirked. Uncertainty gripped me as the footsteps behind me got louder. There was a recess immediately to my right and within I could see the beginnings of a descending staircase.

I scrambled for this opening, leaping down several steps at a time. Uncouth laughter echoed in my ears from above as I went deeper, the staircase winding one, two, three complete circles into the darkness, though flickering wall lanterns gave me just enough light to judge each landing. It became warmer and an indescribable stench rose from somewhere below. Still I leapt three and four steps at a time, certain I had outfoxed the stupid-looking guards, certain also that there would be some escape from these depths to the outside world. The stone became chilly and slightly damp on my one bare sole, even while the air around me grew hotter. Suddenly my bare foot slipped, scooping me at high speed into the air. My hips crashed hard upon a jagged step-ridge. I cried out, fearing my back was broken. Before I had even a chance to gauge the level of pain, a pair of enormous hands grabbed my shoulders and hauled me to my feet.

"You fool!" spat the young guard. I could smell him at close quarters and had to close my eyes from this as much as from the pain. "Do you want to be sent to limbo?"

I could hear other footsteps rattling down the staircase after us and we were washed in an undulating golden light. "What happened?" said the woman who had served me. She had taken one of the lanterns from the wall and now held it close as she peered at us. "Did she fall?"

"We'll have to tell the governor now," murmured the guard in reply. "She's been seen by the guards upstairs, as well as here." He kept his hands on my shoulders and looked down into the dungeon space below us. Still trembling with pain, I followed his gaze.

The first thing I saw was a rat perched upon the side of a ridge two steps below. It nodded its head once or twice to get the measure of the distance it meant to jump. Raising its haunches and sliding its pink hands down the wall, it plunged, landing with a little thud on a bed of straw, dark soil, and rags. But the rags moved suddenly and the shifting became general, every inch of ground in movement. Rats scurried along this surface but the ground itself heaved, gasped, and moaned to the accompaniment of grinding iron.

The pain in my back was entirely gone, replaced by something else—a rebellion of senses. The floor was made up of people. Every bit of it was limb, neck, torso. A hundred dull eyes caught the flame. They either gazed with indifference or looked away in some fever or mute entreaty. This was the source of the stench which hovered around the guard and the serving woman. Just as a demon is supposed to smoke with sulphurous fumes, so the people here were infected with this scent of the damned.

"What's the matter?" called a man on a stone platform enclosed with iron railings. I had not seen this dark elevation which overlooked the many-headed torment below. There was a heavy, iron-studded door behind this guard, and chains and whips at his feet.

"Nothing," answered my guard. "A young prisoner from the master's side. She wandered away. Nothing serious."

"The master's side!" called the man with a laugh. "Don't she know when she has it good?"

A great moan came up from the heaving mass below his feet. The man picked up a whip and lashed it in the air.

"Better get her out of here before she stirs them all up," said the man.

"I better had," the guard mumbled. His hand slipped from my shoulder and held me like a vise above my elbow. We began ascending the staircase, the serving woman first with the lantern, then myself and the guard. With each step I felt all the fight draining from me. A rank vapour rose from the dungeon below and I noticed more rats scurrying about our feet, their whiskers busy as they sniffed the air. A sickly feeling swelled in my stomach like seafoam and I tried to swallow it down.

It occurred to me suddenly that my home was likely to remain within the thick and unmovable walls of this prison for a long time to come. I realized too that the smirk of the guard upstairs and his laughter were not as contemptibly stupid as I thought. They knew what I did not yet know, that the idea of escape was so futile, it was comical.

I was no longer the warrior savage with the lioness's heart. I was a thirteen-year-old girl locked within a vast, stinking maze of a prison. What is more, I had blown away any trust I had on a pointless and ill-conceived rebellion. I would not easily be trusted again.

CHAPTER EIGHT

Have you heard of limbo before, young girl?" Mr. Jarvis asked. It was evening now and the candle flame leapt as it burned, sending a honeyed hue all over the craters of his forehead. He had not stopped scratching with his quill since I entered his office, and gave me only a sidelong glance as he asked me this question. I was standing in exactly the same place as I had been that morning—at the end of the long table— only this time I was flanked on one side by the serving woman and on the other by the prison guard, Gilbert, who had pursued me all the way from my cell to the vile dungeon below. The presence of both these people was oddly comforting as I struggled for an answer.

"I have heard the word only one time, sir," I said.

My voice was very meek and it seemed to please Mr. Jarvis. He leant back in his creaking chair and turned towards me. The hint of a smile played upon his lips.

"Are you a penitent then, girl? Have you seen the error of your ways?"

He laid down his quill.

In reality, I felt far more fear than penitence. Penitence required free will; I remember that from the schoolroom. But I nodded and breathed, "Yes."

Mr. Jarvis sighed, apparently satisfied. "Penitence, yes penitence," he whispered back to me with a mild, longing smile. Then he tapped the desk nervously with his fingers. "You have put me into a very awkward position, young lady." He took a sharp breath. "Your mother's pleas, and your stepfather's great mercy and forbearance have seen to it that you have received the very best a young woman of your character and crimes could hope for." He paused, his pale eyes flickering in the candle. "Tyburn gallows are in constant use. Witchery and seduction keep the city's rope makers and carpenters fully employed." His speech was faster now, his mood agitated. "Yet you," he continued, raising his voice, "you were brought here, given your own room, good food, a straw bed. Yes, you were brought here because your mother and stepfather believed there was hope for you." He stared at me with indignant eyes, as though realizing for the first time the gravity of my great crime.

I hoped he might remain silent for a while. His own words had provoked him to anger just as a gust of wind might tease a flame to the delirious joys of destruction. I watched him shift in his chair, helpless to stall the change coming over him, powerless to prevent him fanning his own flames.

"Do you know what you stumbled across when you ran down that staircase?" he asked in a voice calmer than I expected.

"No sir," I whispered.

"That place we call limbo," Mr. Jarvis said, his expression struggling between bitterness and mirth. "Limbo, child." His mouth turned down at the corners but his eyes formed an odd, teary smile. "You might think this place is merely a prison." He held my gaze. "Do you think that, girl?"

The question carried such weight, and he seemed so intent to hear my reply, that I hesitated. The serving woman coughed slightly and I took this as a warning to hurry. As there were only two possible answers, I took a chance.

"Yes," I said.

His lips twitched. "You think yes," he replied hoarsely. "You think this is just a prison?" Mr. Jarvis cast his gaze around the walls and ceiling. Then his lips and eyes for once synchronized and broke together into a crooked smile. "Well, you are wrong."

I relaxed a little, knowing this was the answer he had wanted from me.

"Newgate is modelled after the plan of the Almighty," he continued. "There is comfort for the loved and for the sorrowful, reward and succour for those who grieve. There are chains, whips, and torments for those without remorse. And," he paused for a moment before whispering, "there is another place. A place for the Jew who circumcises Christians. A place for the pagan who desecrates the altar. A place for the whore who infects royal blood." Mr. Jarvis's lips had become wet, and he dabbed them with his handkerchief. "We have done our best here, young woman, to copy the Divine Plan. We could not devise a hell to match the one all men fear, but limbo is our best attempt. It is quite within my power to send you there."

My knees buckled instantly and I must have been lost for a while. Everything was dim and swirling as though viewed through a fast-flowing stream, and I had the vague idea of scuffing furniture and strong hands about my arms and shoulders. I was on the floor looking up. The pale ceiling swished and circled like an ocean wave, crashing. I was hauled onto feet which could neither feel nor grip the floor, and finally lowered into a chair.

When the pieces of my world reunited into one whole and the room tipped into balance, I found myself looking up at Mr. Jarvis. The governor now stood with his hands behind his back, staring down at me in panicky displeasure. When he saw I was coming to myself again, he stooped forward. From such close quarters I could see his pale eyes were dotted with red.

"I didn't say I was going to send you there," he said, exasperated. "I just said it was quite within my power to do so." The guard and the serving woman were on either side of me again, but I remained on the chair. Mr. Jarvis was breathing heavily. "I know every ploy, young woman, and if I suspect a trick in your fainting spell, it will be the worse for you."

The unnatural privilege of sitting made me nervous, so when the governor nodded to Gilbert and Gilbert's hand came under my elbow, I was relieved to stand. "It was no trick, I assure you, sir. I am ashamed of my fall."

The governor looked at Gilbert as though for confirmation of this. Apparently satisfied, he backed off somewhat awkwardly, regaining his chair without taking his eyes from me.

"You cannot return to your comfortable cell though," he said after a deep breath, "not without appropriate punishment and conclusive proof of your remorse. You must stare ungodliness in the face and tell your keepers here that you recognize and renounce the works of Satan." He looked first at Gilbert, then at the serving woman. Finally, his eyes came to rest upon me. "What is the most evil profession in the world, girl?"

I thought back over his previous speech. "A Jew, sir. A Jew who circumcises Christians."

Mr. Jarvis shook his head as though I were a mosquito trying to land in his ear. "That's not a profession."

"A whore, then, sir. A whore who tries to infect the royal blood."

Mr. Jarvis frowned deeply. "I mean a profession of men, not of women."

"A priest who defiles his own altar."

"No!" Mr. Jarvis snaps, springing from his seat in sudden anger. "The theatre, young woman, the theatre! That is the most ungodly profession of them all. The theatre is a place of debauchery and sin, a place where people dance and strut upon the stage." He cut a rapid two-step caper to make the point. He looked ridiculous enough, but was far too furious to laugh at. "A place where men dress as women and profess their love to other men. It is a place of false oaths and unwholesome stories, a place where commonality drink, fight, and fornicate. It is the theatre that spreads London's plagues and gives rise to the city's moral torpor."

"Yes," I said. "Of course."

The governor looked at me, suspicious.

"What would you say, young woman, if I told you of a play recently confiscated, a play depicting rebellion and the assassination of a king?"

"I'd say it was a good thing—"

"What?" he yelled before I had a chance to finish.

"—that it was confiscated!" I stressed quickly. "A good thing you stopped it from being performed." My heart was thumping. However irrational it was, the governor's fury could lead me to the hell I had stumbled into when I tried to escape. I knew I would be dancing on live embers until I was safely away from him.

"This play went further than the spilling of royal blood," he continued, rubbing his hands together. His voice was hushed now and a knotted vein stood out on his temple. Each word he spoke was like a log to a fire, teasing out an anger that was always fresh, always renewing. "In place of Christian worship there was pagan barbarity. Its characters sought advice not from respectable members of the clergy, but from a coven of witches. What do you think of that? What do you think of the fact that such a spectacle might have played out to the masses a stone's throw from the centre of this great Christian country?"

His lip trembled as he looked up at me.

"I think it a great scandal, sir."

"A scandal, you say, yes!" His pale eyes came alive in the candle flame. "But worse than a scandal! An outrage! This play is an insult to our dear Sovereign Queen and Defender of the Faith!"

"Indeed, sir," I agreed. "An outrage to our dear Queen."

The more his passion rose, the more the governor seemed to forget who I was. He was willing me to concur, visibly comforted when I did.

"And where, I might ask, if you were the governor of Newgate prison, where would you place the villain who had scribbled such a treason and planned for its public performance?"

"In limbo, of course."

"Of course!" he exclaimed, holding his fists in front of his chest and shaking them in triumph. "In limbo, of course. You have said it!" He grinned broadly at me, his eyes filling with tears. "How correct you are!"

Then his mood changed again. His lips became pursed and he stooped over his desk, shuffling letters. "But I am not permitted. Can you believe that?" He glanced up, sniffed, then sat down. "He has influential friends in the city—debauched and disreputable courtiers who frequent the playhouses, and keep the company of such vermin. My hand has been stayed."

"It is a great pity," I said, my confidence growing.

I could hardly blame myself for a little hubris. A few minutes ago I was being threatened with limbo. Now I felt like the governor's closest confidante. I could feel the confusion of my companions who guarded me.

"My whip is fastened," Mr. Jarvis added mournfully. He gazed into the candle flame bobbing on his desk. "My claws are pulled. But," he said brightening, "I can use his presence to reclaim another."

"A good idea, sir." I said.

The governor looked up at me and smiled. "I don't know whether the devil prompts you to such subtle and persuasive answers, young woman. But I mean to find you out." He gazed at me with the same mild expression for some moments, then continued. "I told you I would make you stare ungodliness in the face and renounce the works of Satan. I need to know there is hope for you, that you are young enough to be purged of the evil that infected you in Ireland."

"What are you going to do with me?" I asked. My legs began to tremble again and I felt Gilbert move in closer, preparing to catch my fall.

"I cannot send the playwright to limbo. He is in the least comfortable quarters on the master's side; that is all I've dared to do to him. But I could make things less comfortable for him by sending you to share his cell."

He watched me keenly, anticipation lighting up his face.

I was not sure what to feel and had an idea that lack of protest would disappoint him. So I tried to look worried. And sure enough, he smiled and leaned back slowly.

"You will be in a pit of a different kind," he said, clasping his hands over his stomach. "No chains, no whips, no living carpet of rats. Just another mind, like yours, infected with witchery and corruption." He gazed at me a moment longer. "If you can withstand the horrors of his imagination, I will send a satisfactory report to your parents and you might be permitted to remain on the master's side. If he infects you with his wickedness, you may indeed be sent to limbo." He nodded to the guard. "Take her to the playwright's cell."

CHAPTER NINE

Y ou haven't been out all day, have you?" The question
comes from nowhere, burning its way through my sleep
like a comet. I open my eyes to see a young girl staring
down at me. My dream—and it was a pleasant dream, full of
warm, safe forests carpeted with pine needles, whispering leaves,
and the scent of tree bark and wildflowers—fizzles away into
nothing.

The girl is holding a candle in front of her face. Her hair is golden,
her eyes green. There was a time when I used to see such a creature
gazing at me from the mirror of my parents' house in the Pale.

I know this must be Emma Rose.

"That's curious, isn't it?" she continues, while I push myself up
from the mattress. I see there is a smaller child next to her.
"Everyone else has been frantic." Emma tilts her head to one side.
"What do you think about that, Mary? You and I, Mother and
Father, the whole settlement, have been running around, searching

and calling, driving ourselves mad while this old woman sleeps in her clothes on her stinking bed."

Mary looks up at her older sister, her eyes as wide as saucers. She shrinks away from me a little.

"And I heard a curious thing," Emma continues, clearly not expecting any answer from her younger sister. "Mother telling Aunt about something this old woman said, something about how Sara had never come to visit her. That is odd, isn't it, since Sara told me she intended to come up here and confront the old witch?"

"How long have you been standing there?" I ask the child, trying hard to sound more angry than frightened. But there is a quaver in my voice.

"Long enough to tire of your snoring," Emma answers.

Emma, like her sister Sara, shows not the slightest sign of fear or self-doubt. Also, like her sister, she is pretty with perfect rosy cheeks. What I would not give to slap them! But I do nothing; I know she holds all the power.

"What do you want from me?" I ask quietly.

"Information, for a start."

"Information about what?" I ask.

"Why, about the disappearance of my sister, of course."

"I don't know anything about that," I say quickly. It was convincing enough, but I can feel my heart beating. I am trapped, and merely wish for this all to be over. Burn me, hang me, but get me out of this unnatural situation.

"Oh, I think you do know, old woman."

Suddenly, my sinews tighten and the fear falls away from me like water running off from a breeched awning. "It's Sheila, not 'old woman,' and I don't care what you think you know. Get out of my cabin."

Emma takes a step backwards as though reading my intentions. I was indeed about to strike her.

"There's no need for that," she says, smiling. "If I'd wanted to give you away, we could have done so already."

"What do you want, then?" I swing my legs to the floor and raise myself into a standing position.

"I told you. Information."

Emma takes a sideways step as I make for my chair. She pulls her sister with her as though she were a rag doll.

"I told you I don't know about Sara," I say, lowering myself onto the chair.

"Oh, I don't care about that, although I have to admit I'm curious."

I stare at the girl's smiling face for a moment. Mary is still frightened. She sucks her thumb and nestles into her older sister.

"You don't care?"

"No, why should I?" she asks briskly. "We didn't really get on, you know. Well," she adds with a smirk, her speech slowing, "if I'm honest, it's not entirely true to say I don't care. I do, but not in the usual way. I care that she's gone because it makes my life so much easier. Looking for two wealthy husbands to take on the business will be much easier for my father than looking for three. And as you can see, I'm the older and I'm very pretty, so I should have the best chance." She smiles a little more broadly and wrinkles her brow. "What are you looking at me like that for?"

I am not aware of looking at her in any particular way, but I know I am in shock, and have been, perhaps, since the moment of my awakening. I never thought I could come across a young woman more arrogant or cruel than Sara Rose. But here is such another before me, in a form even more angelic, the candlelight playing on her golden curls, her green eyes like a calm sea at sunset.

"I know what you're thinking. What a little monster! Everyone thinks that about me, except for Mother and Father, of course. They adore me. But it's just as well I am a little monster, isn't it? If I weren't, I'd have already told everyone about Sara going to see you last night."

"You don't know that," I venture. She seemed to imply as much earlier, and I don't want to be at this girl's mercy.

"Not absolutely conclusively, no. I know she intended to come and see you. And I know she's missing now. I would be worried about that if I were you."

"And how will you explain your own silence up to now?"

"Oh, when your name is mentioned, Sheila, you may be sure my father will forget every other detail."

"Why?"

Already I wished I had not spoken.

"Oh, you've no idea! He's terrified of you! He has nightmares about you."

Something in my chest rolls like a battle drum.

"What kind of man is terrified of an old woman?" I say. Mary cowers into her sister. Emma merely smiles as before. "What have I ever done to him?"

"Pathetic, isn't it?" says Emma. "A grown man!" Then she laughs out loud. "And him so holy, so respected . . . There you go, staring at me again! I'm supposed to live in this place with nothing but rock and ocean and uncouth boys with broken teeth, yet I'm supposed to be sorry when my chances of escape suddenly increase twofold or more. And I've got a father who wails in the night of the witch who will destroy him, and I'm supposed to honour him like it says in the Bible. Even you expect me to do so—the witch herself wants me to respect such a man!"

Emma lets go of her sister and collapses onto my bed in laughter, the candle wavering in her hand. Mary comes close to the bed and her sister's side; she throws me terrified glances.

"You see," says Emma, noticing this, "Mary's frightened of you too!" She tugs her little sister's shawl until Mary sits down beside her on the bed.

"What do you want from me?" I ask, repeating the only question that may get this girl out of my cabin.

Emma stops laughing at last. She clears her throat and stares at me hard. "I want to know about Mary and me."

"What about you?"

"My father is convinced the Roses are cursed, that they will never have male children."

"Yes," I say wearily, throwing my eyes to the ceiling.

And as subtle as a twitch of a bird's feather, Emma catches it.

"You've heard this story before," she says, her gaze steady in the candlelight, her face fixed like marble. "I wondered about that."

"How could I have done?" I say, but my cheeks are burning and I know it is too late.

"My mother is very nervous, isn't she? You'd think that would make her more careful to make sure she isn't followed."

"What are you talking about?"

"Don't lie about Mother coming to visit you or I'll know for certain you're lying about Sara too."

I take in a slow breath.

"Well, what about it?"

"The way it stands now, I and my little sister here could do quite well off this curse. It makes us my father's heirs. We might make some kind of marriage that can get us to another place in return for the business."

"What are you worried about, then?"

"Oh, we're worried that the curse will lift, that Mother may be with child already. I have heard her retching in the morning. If she is with child, it's vital to us the baby not be a boy. A boy would be a little prince, and all Father's favour and energy would be devoted to him. I could forget about an advantageous marriage then, couldn't I? Father would already have his heir."

"You must know your mother is too old to be with child," I say quickly. But I can feel my eyelids batter and I can see the disbelief on the girl's face.

"It would be very foolish to try to lie to me again," Emma says quietly, holding the candle very still. "I'm the only friend you've got."

I know I am undone this time. My confidences must be spilled to this girl like fish guts to the knife. She holds me utterly in her power. "Yes," I say with a sigh, "she's pregnant, and I don't know whether the curse will be lifted. I tried. I told her I thought it would work, but I'm not sure."

Emma jumps off the bed and tugs on Mary's dress. The little sister follows. "Good," she says. "I was going to set light to your bed if you'd told another lie. It would have spread and burned your cabin down in no time at all. I'm glad you decided to trust me."

She leads Mary around me and gains the doorway. "All I'll ask for now is that you keep me informed about Mother. Tell me as soon as you know the sex of her child. I may require your help."

She opens the door, turns back, and smiles at me oddly.

"Do you believe my parents are cursed?"

It takes me a while to answer. The girl's expression, though frivolous, challenges me again to be truthful.

"Not the way your mother thinks, no," I find myself saying.

I thought Emma would not understand my meaning. However much I dislike her, I have no wish to insult the person who holds my fate in her hands. But it's obvious straight away that she does understand. Far from being insulted, my admission has had the opposite effect. The girl's eyes glisten with delight.

"I know exactly what you mean," she says. "What could my parents have done to deserve such children? That's what you are thinking. With what manner of changelings have they been burdened?"

She stares at me for a moment longer. Then, grabbing hold of Mary's hand, she lets out a laugh and disappears with her candle through the open door.

I am left in darkness.

————

I drop the last of the firewood David Butt collected into the hearth. Tomorrow it will be gone and I must start to forage again. The very idea makes my bones ache and I would like to save some fuel. But tonight I must stay warm, as I cannot sleep. Emma Rose has murdered sleep.

The sentence stops me for a moment. I hold from striking the flint again so my thoughts can settle. Apt though it is, the idea of "murdering sleep" isn't mine. I crouch in darkness, allowing this echo to lead me back to its source. I find myself sitting on a hard stone floor in a small damp cell. The playwright's cell is much worse than my original room in Newgate, but it surprises me how much I appreciate the company. I could do with a cellmate now, rather than the odd parade of people who come and go like characters in a nightmare. I think of my former prison companion and wonder how long he lived. He's bound to be long dead by now, of course, or else he'd be more than a hundred years old. Everyone from my golden years is gone. The only companions I have now are the dry sticks at my feet. I strike the flint hard and the twigs take. Smoke wafts up as I poke the burning stick ends under the pile. My chest heaves as I cough, splutter, and cough again.

The room takes on the gold of the flame and, as if my hearing were awakened by light, I distinctly catch a plaintive call of "Sara . . . Sa-ra" from below. The sound, I realize, has been there all the time, as constant and as unnoticed as my own breathing.

Mr. Jarvis's description of ungodliness and sedition had prepared me for something more than the harmless-looking man whose cell I was to share.

I was worried enough when the guard, Gilbert, gripped my upper arm with one hand and unlocked the cell door with the other. The clank of the lock sent reverberations through my heart. The guard pushed open the door and made a bit of a show of hauling me roughly into the cell, though his heart wasn't in it—I could tell—

and his grip was rather loose. When I had got my bearings, I turned to see the playwright sitting on a blanket in the corner.

"What's this?" he asked the guard. He frowned at my presence as though surveying a mangy animal he had been asked to purchase.

My first thought on looking him over was one of amazement that such a slight and insubstantial creature should have so upset a man like the governor, so full of power and importance. My second thought was one of indignation that his looks and words should have disparaged me before I had had the chance to disparage him.

"Governor's orders. She's to share with you."

The stranger looked at me once more and groaned. Then he gazed up to the tiny barred window through which daylight scattered. "You took away a hundred faithful bedfellows and replace them with only one. Why must you cut me off so savagely from all society?"

"What nonsense is this?" the serving woman demanded. "You had no company before."

"The blanket of which you robbed me, madam, housed so many fleas that each night seemed an orgy."

"None of your filth!" she snapped. "You should be glad we took the blanket away if it was infested. If we'd known you were using the tiny creatures to gratify yourself, we would have taken it away earlier."

The stranger raised his eyebrows and smiled at me.

The serving woman looked in my direction. "I'll be bringing food for both of you later on," she said. "Everything will work out fine," she added softly.

"Thank you," said the playwright, waving at them both and

smiling in an exaggerated fashion. "Thank you so much for not starving us!"

The serving woman gave the playwright one more forbidding look and followed Gilbert from the cell. The door clunked shut. Then came the sound of the bolt being drawn. I remained where I was, not more than four yards from the stranger. For a moment there was not the slightest sound. Then the playwright drew up his knees slowly and clasped his hands together in a steeple.

"Well," he said without taking his eyes from the window. "What manner of jape in life's comic dance brings you to Newgate prison?"

I backed away to the opposite corner and sat down. "It's not a joke and I don't find it funny."

He lowered his gaze to meet mine. An earring almost lost in the curls of his reddish hair lent him a roguish look his delicate frame could not quite sustain. Thin lines formed about his eyes as his lips curled into a smile. His was a face accustomed to laughter, it seemed, and the thought scared me. If ordinary things like humour could exist here, this meant people must cease to see the horror around them. In turn, that meant they saw this place as home.

"Oh, but you are wrong," he said with a hoarse laugh. "We must take what merriment we can. Life makes little sense if you try to take it too seriously."

I had never met a playwright before, but even at thirteen I found this man fitting into my preconceived notions—his affectation, his inability to see things as they are, as though life were only a performance. "That's nonsense," I said. "I do take it seriously and I hate being here. So should you."

"You know that I am a poet and a playwright?" he asked with quiet pride.

"Yes," I replied sullenly. "They told me."

"Know, then, that I view misfortune differently from most people." He gazed at the steeple of his hands as he spoke. "I've come to see life itself as a play, a play with random and unplanned scenes." His voice rose dramatically and he paused for an instant before continuing. "Life is like a tale told by an idiot, signifying nothing."

"When *you* write about it, I suppose it must be."

His face showed some surprise. But he was too arrogant to be insulted.

"How old are you?" he asked.

"Thirteen," I answered, looking at him askance.

"And what are you doing here?"

"I don't know," I mumbled.

"You must have some idea."

"Maybe I do, but I'm not going to tell you, am I?"

"I don't see why not," he said, tilting his head and trying to make me out. "I'll tell you my story if you tell me yours."

"I know your story already," I replied, picking at the straw near my foot.

"Fame at last! Even if it's fame within these cursed walls, it's better than the pit of oblivion."

"I don't see it's anything to be proud of, writing about witchcraft and assassination."

He smiled again, reversing his steeple and turning his palms upwards to examine them. "I didn't write about witchcraft and assassination," he replied quietly. "I wrote about the corrupting power of ambition. Never mistake the cover for the book." He smiled to himself, still gazing at the lines on his palms.

His evasions made me restless and irritable. I twisted a straw in my fingers. "They told me you had witches in place of clergy and that a rightful king was slain."

"Oh, yes. It was a story from Scottish history. A nobleman, Macbeth, murdered the king Duncan, concealed the crime, and became king himself."

"So it *is* about assassination."

The playwright breathed in very slowly, then smacked his lips. "No, I told you," he said, "I write beyond the details. Events are only important for what they reveal in men's hearts."

"You're just playing with words," I said.

The playwright closed his eyes for a moment and gave a bitter, soundless laugh. "Why won't you tell me your crime?" he asked. "Did you murder someone? Am I safe here with you?"

He didn't smile but I could tell he was joking, and the question made me relax a little.

"They think I'm a witch or something," I said.

"Who does?" he asked.

"My parents . . . my mother and stepfather."

"Why?"

"Because of Ireland. They think the forest infected me with evil."

"No, what incident caused them to turn you in? Something must have happened."

I had been twisting a straw around one of my fingers, thinking quite beyond the words I spoke, about Thomas Ridley's red lips and sandy hair. Suddenly I realized the straw was around my fourth finger and resembled a wedding ring. I pulled it quickly from my finger and let it fall. "My stepbrother," I said, feeling my face burn. "They found us together."

"Ah," the playwright said thoughtfully. "For how long had you lived together?"

"A few weeks. My mother only just remarried."

"Ah," he said, as though he had discovered something.

"What do you mean, 'ah'?" I demanded.

He ignored my question and asked his own.

"How long has your father been dead?"

"Not long. Scarcely two months. Why?"

"Why? Because the more guilty people feel, the more likely they are to accuse others."

"What does that mean?"

"It means that your mother and your stepfather cannot endure the idea that you are judging them."

"I'm not judging him." I shook my head, wishing we had not started on this. "You don't know anything about it. What kind of fool ends up in prison for writing a play anyway?"

"What kind of thirteen-year-old ends up in prison?" He seemed amused again. "As you are less than half my age, you must be more than twice the fool; you have achieved the same degree of folly in less than half the time."

I stared at him hard for a few moments, then looked away, gazing up towards the window.

We were silent for a while. I thought of Thomas, trying to picture what he'd be doing now. Was he remonstrating with his father, or somewhere in the prison offices below, perhaps, arguing to gain my freedom? Try as I could, I failed to picture Thomas locking horns with Mr. Ridley or Mr. Jarvis; in either case it would be like a feather doing battle with a stone.

A movement from the corner interrupted my thoughts. Something had stirred under the straw. The playwright pulled some crumbs out of his pocket and whistled softly. I glanced over to see two black eyes and a quivering snout emerge from under the straw. "Looks like I must seek out what company I may," the playwright said softly, whistling again and bouncing the crumbs upon his palm. "We two are not the only fools."

I wanted to remain angry with the playwright, but there was so little else to do. The rat was large and grey when it fully emerged. As it approached, then scurried away, stood on its hind legs, sniffed the air, and squeaked, the creature excited first my attention and, before very long, something else. Its shining eyes and eagerness drew tender pity from some deep well inside me.

The playwright threw a crumb, which the rat caught in its pink hands. "We three sages will dine and sup each night together," he told the animal, "and talk of the world beyond this prison; who rises, who falls, who wins, who loses."

"I never said anything against my stepfather," I said sullenly. "He couldn't think I was judging him, because I gave no clue."

I thought too much time had passed for the playwright to remember how our conversation had stalled, and I felt foolish for starting again at the same point, but I didn't know how else to join the odd camaraderie taking place in the cell.

"Oh, do you like him, then?" the playwright asked quietly, holding out another crumb, trying to get the rat to come closer.

"No."

"And do you like the fact your recently widowed mother has married him?"

"No, of course not."

"Well, then, unless you are a very much better actor than you appear, your very presence judges them. Is that not so?"

I stared down at the straw by my feet. This time, I had to admit, he had a point.

CHAPTER TEN

I s it my judgment that Simon Rose fears? Do I hold a blade
of condemnation over his quivering form, as I did over my
mother and Mr. Ridley, without even knowing it? I listen to
the crackling fire and try to imagine the workings of a mind still
plagued by nightmares after more than forty years of life, a mind
so terrified of an old woman that approaching her is out of the
question—even when a loved one goes missing, even when the
old woman may hold some particle of information about the disappearance. What would my playwright companion have made of
such a creature? What demons of guilt or fear must cower within such a breast?

The plaintive search still goes on in the darkness beyond. I
hear footfalls in the forest, the snapping of twigs, men calling to
each other. They have given up calling her name. Soon dawn will
lift the veil of night, and any forlorn hopes lurking in the darkness will scatter into comfortless day. The searchers will realize

the lost one has slipped beyond reclamation. They will return to their homes to plan for more searches, but hope will have gone from them.

A rustle of leaves and the scuff of wood—something stirs outside, very close to my door. My heart stops as I turn from the fire. Simon Rose has come! He has braved the night at last because he suspects I know what happened to Sara. Perhaps Emma has told him about her sister's visit and my own lie.

The door slowly creaks open and I rise, my breath suspended. But Elizabeth Rose, not Simon, slips in. She closes the door, her movements deft and silent as a lizard's.

"I couldn't knock," she says quietly, her large eyes blinking in the glow of the firelight. "They might have heard." She goes over to the bed and sits. "We haven't found her. I knew we wouldn't."

"But it's not even a full day yet," I say, recovering my breath. "When the daylight comes you will find your Sara."

Elizabeth gives a nervous smile. "Emma told me everything about her visit," she says quietly.

My legs turn to lead. I daren't try to sit; any movement might cause my collapse.

"You've no idea how grateful I am to you," she says, glancing up at me. The firelight shines golden pools in her eyes and I see they are filling with tears.

"Grateful?" The weight of uncertainty drags me down at last; I collapse upon the chair and grip its edges with my fingers.

"Emma is so sensitive. She feels things more deeply than you can imagine."

Blood rushes around my ears so fast, her words are muffled.

Yet I understand the danger is passing. Whatever Emma has told her mother, it is nothing that will damn me.

"She told me how you comforted her and Mary," Elizabeth continues. "Poor Emma is so distraught about Sara. I don't know how she'll take it when it's clear that all is lost."

I run my hand over my forehead, trying to fathom what Elizabeth has said.

Emma, sensitive and distraught? I, a comfort to her? I have a sudden vision of Emma: Each of her hands holds the strings of a puppet. One of the puppets has the large eyes and delicate frame of Elizabeth Rose. The other is an ancient and hag-ridden creature like myself.

"I let Emma and Mary know I was with child. I had to tell them something that would ease the pain of their sister's loss. Emma made me promise to come to you often as the baby grows inside me. She said you were so wise and sympathetic, you would ensure a happy outcome. "

"Of course," I say hoarsely. I am beginning to see there are worse things than detection, and that my unwitting role in Sara's death, and even the lies I told afterwards, may be easier to own up to than the crimes that lay ahead. There is a pit yawning for me, a downward pathway to betrayal and self-disgust if I remain at the mercy of Emma Rose. Something rumbles inside my chest, a primal warning to extricate myself from this fate.

"But Simon is the problem now," Elizabeth whispers.

"What about him?" I ask.

"He thinks you are responsible for Sara's death."

The hammer-blow comes with sickening power. A minute ago, when Elizabeth first entered and I was braced for any onslaught, nothing happened. Now that I am tired and slackened with relief, it hits me. And it hits with such force I can feel my secrets spilling like caplin teeming from a broken net. It is relief that sweeps over me as I part my lips to speak.

"Elizab—"

"You mustn't blame him too much," she interrupts with some passion, "although I see it must hurt." I hold off for a moment. It seems I was mistaken; she does not concur with her husband. "Simon is the most superstitious man I have ever known," she continues, her tone almost a plea. "It's part of his faith, you see, his tendency to see monsters lurking in every shadow. In the day-time he's a man true and brave, but at night his courage scatters like the sand. It's his burden. As spiritual leader he has to be more sensitive than other men . . ." Her speech trails away, and she seems embarrassed for a moment. "Simon's father told him a story about you," she continues. "When I mentioned you tonight, he told me again, in more detail than before. His fear of you is fresher than ever."

Elizabeth pauses, looking down thoughtfully, the flames reflected on her pale cheeks. I wait, not making a sound. "His father told him that every child has a guardian angel who comforts them and looks out for them until they are grown."

"That's nothing to be afraid of," I say.

Elizabeth holds out her hand to let her finish. "His father also told him that some unlucky children have an evil spirit."

"An evil spirit?" I repeat.

Elizabeth nods and continues through tightened lips. "An evil spirit whose job it is to find a way through the guardian angel's defences and harm the child. Unlike the guardian angel, such a spirit appears as human and makes its home close to the child it wishes to harm."

"This is madness! Why would a father fill his child's head with such wicked nonsense?"

Elizabeth shakes her head. "I don't know, but he isn't free of it, even now. You see, you and Simon came to our settlement at the same time. This was part of the legend my father-in-law repeated to Simon. The evil spirit comes newly to a settlement with the arrival of the child it haunts."

"I was unlucky indeed, then, to come when I did," I say, trembling with quiet anger, "so soon after Simon's mother gave birth."

"No, Simon's mother did not bear him," Elizabeth says, looking suddenly tired. "He was found."

"Found? Where?"

"Simon's father wanted it never to be talked about, and rarely is it mentioned, although, of course, all the elders know." She smiles, glancing at me. "And in a way, it's helped Simon as community leader." She pauses and sighs. "You see, he was found in a boat drifting off into the bay while John Rose was fishing. John brought the baby home and had his wife nurse him as his own son. He became very protective, too much so, perhaps; he had wanted a boy for so long." Elizabeth laughs fondly for a second so that the tiredness and grief almost lift from her heavy eyes. "They made a great deal, John and his wife, about how Simon was found. Privately, of course. John told Simon he was like Moses who the Bible tells us was found in the bulrushes and, like Moses, he too was certain to be a great leader of his people."

"But why would he want to make the child fear me? How is that helping to build a past for him?"

"You were the stranger, I suppose. To John's fevered mind you must have been a threat." I stare at Elizabeth and, as I can see pity in her face, I know she must see the hurt in mine. "Is it not possible," she asks, "that a woman who has lost everything—husband, children, grandchildren—can be a threat to a man in his position? Is it not possible that a woman with nothing may stake claim to an orphan child?"

"For *this*, I was ostracized?" I gasp. "For *this*, I was kept away?"

"Many elders said that you too preferred it that way. That you were too wounded to be part of the day-to-day life of the settlement."

I consider this for a moment.

"It's true I hardly noticed the people around me and I did not mind them staying away. Any wounded animal retreats. It is nature. But the settlement should not have encouraged me to hide."

"No, we should not have encouraged you," Elizabeth whispers. "But it is too late now."

I give a soft, bitter laugh. How might things have been if John Rose had not arranged for me to live away from the settlement? Would I have aged into the same old woman? Would I be so despised now if the hush of tragedy and suspicion had not hung about my dwelling all these years? Would I be the feared and wizened creature I am now if I had drawn from the settlement below the love and laughter of the inhabitants as well as their secrets and shames? It's as if, through long practice, I have learned to maintain a private conduit to these people's nightmares. Their darkness has fed into mine until my morbid tendencies have become chronic. I am an unwholesome old woman feeding an unwholesome town. And how can I deny that I led David Butt to murder? I flamed his unrequited passion. I fanned his desire until his own life, and the lives of others, meant nothing to him. Too late, yes. Too late for me. Too late for David Butt. And too late for Sara Rose.

Elizabeth is silent for some time. At last she shifts from my bed and stands.

"I am sorry for your trouble, Sheila."

I give a slow sigh. Part of me still wants to tell her everything, to shed the dark burden of secrecy from my shoulders. Even if the penalty is death, it would at least remind me what it feels like to feel clean and unfettered. But I hold back, and Elizabeth is at my door by the time I answer.

"And I'm sorry for yours."

I catch a sad smile in the firelight and then she is gone.

I sit still in my chair and wait for the dawn.

———

The night passed easily though it was cold. Both of us threw scraps to our new friend who darted and scurried in and out of hiding. The playwright talked a great deal and I hardly noticed the sun rise until our tiny cell was awash in milky light. Against my expectations, some of what he said was quite interesting. He told me of the play for which he had been imprisoned. It sounded vile and ignoble, a foul and infectious story. It would have made me want to send him to prison too, if I'd had power to do so. And yet, it had a quality; there was something in the way he told it— a spiralling dread about what a man might be capable of once he begins on a certain path.

He told me he wrote compulsively and stored up plays for future use, for whenever the company needed them. He usually noted down phrases or sayings he thought clever. When he felt like it—and this could be years after he jotted it down—he might put the words into the mouths of his characters. I thought this sounded like a slapdash way of doing things and I told him so.

"I'll not take the advice of a thirteen-year-old girl whose sole achievement in life so far is to find her way to Newgate prison," he laughed.

"If being in Newgate Prison makes me stupid and ill-prepared for giving advice," I said, "you might want to reflect for a moment and look around. You're not in the Queen's Palace either."

He seemed pleased that I had learned to fence with words.

"Well," he said with an approving smile. "I must be foolish indeed to ask this question of so rapier a wit, but what do you think of the way I told the story?"

"The one about the Scottish King?"

"It's the only one I've told you so far."

"If you think me such a fool, why do you want to know?"

"Fool or not, you are my only audience now."

He shifted on his straw and his face seemed to colour in the dawn light.

"I liked it," I said, knowing it was the answer he wanted.

A smile played about his lips. He put his hand to his face and scratched his beard.

"What did you like about it?" he asked through a yawn which seemed a little contrived.

"I don't know," I said. "Something about a single crime damning a person forever." I paused; my bottom lip had suddenly become heavy as I realized the words might easily pertain to myself.

But the playwright, not noticing my unease, latched onto the praise. "Yes," he said, sitting more upright, "a crime against nature and custom. A crime that curses generations to come. A crime that sends planets spinning off course while bloodshed and mayhem reign below, while men prey upon each other like monsters of the deep."

He became quite intense for a moment, then pursed his lips.

"What else did you like about it?"

I thought for a moment, and tried to make my answer something more specific, and further from myself.

"I suppose it made me know what it would feel like to be responsible for someone's death," I said quietly. "The part about the dagger appearing before the murder. The trouble the murderer and his wife have cleaning off the blood afterwards. It made me understand what a guilty conscience would feel like."

"You should hear the whole play when it's finished and performed."

"Will they ever let you perform it, do you think?"

"Oh yes, one day." He threw a morsel at the rat which had re-emerged hungry with the dawn. "It's just politics and power, that's all. It changes like the tide. I'll have my day again."

He seemed weary for a moment, but then roused himself, running his fingers through his hair. "But too much praise is not good for me. You must tell me what you did not like about the story too."

I was glad he asked me this, because I had some ideas about how it could be improved.

"The ending," I said.

"The ending?" he repeated with a tense smile, tilting his head as though eager to listen.

"The king believed he was indomitable because the witches told him he could not be defeated by one of woman born."

"Yes," he said hastily, his eyes alive with anticipation. "Yes, but he did not know that his adversary, Macduff, was from his mother's womb untimely ripped."

"Yes," I said slowly.

"What a finale it will make!" he enthused, throwing another scrap to the rat. As though infected by the playwright's excitement, the animal leaped to catch the food, its whiskers bristling. "The mystical hand of chance stretching forth to snuff out the candle when arrows and swords have been unable to do so. What did you think of it?"

I don't know why I listened to his words and ignored his clear meaning. I have since come to know that a plea for an honest opinion is really a plea for support and that no one ever wants to hear bad news. I had no idea of this when I spoke.

"It seems like cheating," I said. "Just because the baby was taken from its mother's womb before she gave birth," I continued, "that doesn't mean he wasn't 'born of woman,' does it? He still had a mother. He still grew in her and was delivered from her belly into the world. It seems like you're just playing with words again."

"Playing with words," he repeated, his dark eyes fixing me oddly. The rat stopped eating and turned its head towards me. The playwright chuckled. "Playing with words, the child says." The rat twitched its whiskers. "Do you understand dramatic irony, young woman?" The playwright's voice was soft but infused with disapproval and hurt.

"It's only the ending," I said. "I liked everything else."

I picked up a morsel of bread and threw it towards the rat but the creature scurried away to the corner as though the food were a missile.

The playwright ground his teeth and stared at me. "A play has to be a complete entity," he said. "It must be the be-all and end-all."

I thought for a moment, repeating his words to myself, trying to make sense of them.

"The what?" I asked at last.

"The be-all and end-all, a neat package with no loose ends, a finished story that leaves its audience satisfied."

The playwright was troubled now. I could see perspiration on his forehead.

"Oh," I nodded slowly. "Is that one of your phrases: *the be-all and end-all*? One that you store up for future use?"

He didn't reply at first but closed his eyes and looked up to the window. "Yes," he mumbled hopelessly. "It's one of my phrases."

"It's good," I lied.

The playwright leaned his head back against the wall.

"I think I'll go to sleep for a while," he said, closing his eyes.

It was so sudden I thought it was a joke and that, in a moment, his eyes would open again. But they did not. Save for the soft breathing of my companion, the cell remained still and silent.

I played with the straw at my feet.

CHAPTER ELEVEN

With the dawn comes rain, and along with the constant patter and dribble, something else. Is the fresh presence the chill hovering around my shoulders now the fire has quite burned out? No, it isn't the cold that makes me listen intently and shiver from within. It's silence.

Why should silence disturb me? My mouth becomes dry as I search for an answer, and there is a sickly movement inside my belly. The rain drips and sloshes as it oozes from the sticks and dried grass that make up my eaves, and lands on the mud below.

It is a weekday, but nobody is working. Sara is still gone, but the search for her has ceased.

There is not the slightest room for doubt. Something has happened. Sara Rose's body must have turned up. The community below must be in mourning.

How will it all work out? How obvious are the bruises David Butt left around her neck? It surely won't take long for them to discover that David murdered her and left the settlement to escape punishment.

But slow down. If Sara had turned up dead, would I not have heard a dreadful commotion? I was awake for most of the night, after all. If it had occurred during the short while I was asleep, the noise and activity would surely have roused me.

But the shadow of last night's dream passes over me again and I realize that nightmares can absorb all that surrounds them. My dreams did indeed carry a flavour of unrest. Fires burned on the distant horizon. Cannon smoke billowed into the sky. There were booms and shouts. I saw my daughter Katherine's face as a lean and dun-coloured pirate approached her with a sword. I screamed out so that I might escape this phantasm; I knew too well how it would end. Katherine's hands were on the rim of the small boat and she pushed herself off, ducked from the whistling blade, and then ran along the pebble shoreline skimming water with her toes. I called out again, shut my eyes tight, and held my fists over my ears.

From time to time this happens to me: I find myself on the beach reliving a pure memory in place of a nightmare. This time the scene dissolved as I willed it to. I was in a valley again, not on a beach, and again I was watching a distant battle. Muffled yells were exchanged and I heard the desperate wail of a woman. I did not see the cause of her grief. Everything was smoke and darkness, but somehow I knew her family was being butchered before her eyes.

Suddenly I was back on the beach again. It was some while after the pirate attack. I stared at the waves as they rolled and lapped upon the shore. Drifting in slowly, bobbing on the surface, were blackened planks of driftwood, all that remained of one of our fishing boats that the pirates had set adrift.

When I awoke, my curiosity fixed not upon the unusual violence and horror of the dream but upon the one detail that had always puzzled me: I had seen the pirates set the boats adrift, and I had witnessed them floating away intact upon the random tide. They were still in sight even after the pirate ship had dipped beyond the rim of the world. How, then, did the remains become scorched by fire?

It was this point alone that I pondered while—before the silence struck me, before the yells of a nightmare suggested themselves as real activity below—I listened to the dawn drizzle. Now I am quite certain the dream battle echoed something going on in the settlement. The unseen woman who wailed in desperation may have been Elizabeth Rose, and the distant shouting might have been the general panic that ensued.

How long will I wait before I hear anything? If Elizabeth is in deep mourning, who will tell me? Emma, perhaps, but I cringe when I think of her visit and wonder what new demands it might bring. There are three or four people who might come to me for help in the next few days, but would they take the trouble to keep me informed? And would I want them to? I fear my blushes and wonder at the things people might guess.

Oddly, since I knew her but little until this business between Sara and David, the only person I'd like to talk to is Elizabeth Rose. She seemed to seek me for solace last night. Perhaps it's because I too have been robbed of children. Perhaps it's this grief that brings us closer. I think of last night's conversation with her and I struggle to disentangle her words from the details of my dream. Her husband, Simon, overprotected son of the venerable John Rose, was not born of his mother like other men. Rather he was found while his father was fishing. It sounds like a legend or a nursery tale, and I have to remember Elizabeth's posture as she sat on my bed and the tone of her voice as she related this story. Only these details make me certain I heard it before, and not after, I fell asleep.

The wind outside changes direction; something comes loose from my roof and scatters down from the eaves, landing on the mud. A leak is certain to follow. I grip my chair arms and raise myself up. I hear the *drip, drip, drip* already as water hits my work table then splashes up, leaving a cold kiss upon my forehead. It could be this invasion of the elements that sends me to the door. Recently I have relied on Seth Butt for my repairs. But Seth will have his own troubles with David gone, and I am loath to set foot in the village today.

I draw my shawl over my head and open the door anyway, just to see the woods. The morning is fresh and cool and the leaves and grass stalks tremble under the falling droplets. I step out under the rain, I've no idea why, perhaps my rebellion against waiting. The scent of wet pine draws me towards the trees. I can feel the raindrops seep through my shawl and into my hair. My shoes soak up the puddles, but I'm not concerned. An old woman gets wet. Why should she not? There is no one who will fret about me, and anyway the forest is my friend. I slip between two wet branches, feeling a soft tug upon my shawl. Leaves hiss and scatter at my approach. I remember the words of the man of the forest: *While the woods embrace you, no spirit or beast can harm you, no strangers or neighbours smite you, no dank ague infect you. When death lies all around you, the leaves and boughs protect you.*

I'd rather be damp here under the forest's protection than damp in my own cabin. It's been so long since I've seen the man of the forest I wonder now if he ever existed. It is this, more than any-thing, that draws me forward to walk among the trees. Children, I have heard, are born with the echo of paradise in their ears. It is the place from which we have come and the place to which we hope to return. The soft voice of the man of the forest seemed to promise paradise all those years ago. As the leaves and pine needles yield to my tread and a squirrel scurries out of my way, I remember how I felt then. The world was like a glorious rainbow which I had as yet barely glimpsed. There was endless beauty and limitless joy.

The sun has emerged from the clouds and scatters its way through the leaves overhead. Summer rain glistens in patches, turn-ing spots of undergrowth to gold. The route I have been following is one I often use to collect firewood. I know each fruit tree and every mossy trunk. The breeze stirs again, scattering a shower of droplets from the leaves. These, too, catch the sun and wink like pearls as they fall. There is another noise, from further behind me than the patter of droplets. It sounds like the tread of caribou, only bolder. I hear voices, too. Whoever it is must be very close to my cabin, judging from the sound. I think I hear a door creaking open.

I turn immediately and make my way back through the pliant leaves. If a door did open, it could only be mine—there are no others within earshot. Why would a group of men be opening my door? The question smacks me as rudely as the wet branch which springs back against my forehead. I push it away and hurry along, a coldness clutching my heart. At last the men come into view, their dark shoulders hunched beyond the saplings. They are indeed standing around the open doorway of my cabin.

Parting the saplings with my hands, I press through the undergrowth. As I come out into the open, the men turn towards me. One of them is Seth Butt, his face ashen, his eyes rimmed with red. Another is Elizabeth Rose's cousin, Joshua. He is timid, yet physically strong, with the same reptile eyes as his cousin. The last, a young man with a stalk of hay in his mouth, is Jack Power. He fishes sometimes with Seth and David.

"Well, what is it that you want?" I ask. But I don't want an answer. I tuck my head down and walk an arc around them, making for the door. Joshua shifts half a pace to the side, as though letting me past. But it's just his nerves. Already I have doubts that they mean to let me inside. The silence of spinning thoughts surrounds them; they are like hawks twitching their feathers while they measure the distance to their prey. And sure enough, before I reach the threshold, Seth bounds in front of me, barring me from the door.

I glare at him. His eyes are desperate and afraid.

"Out of my way! Do you want an old woman to die of the damp and cold?"

Seth Butt remains where he is and the other two approach and stand behind each of my shoulders.

"It is natural to fear cold and damp," says Seth, straining the words through gritted teeth. "It is natural to fear the agues sent by Satan to plague mankind. Yet you walk in the dripping forests inviting such misfortune!"

The men at either shoulder have not yet laid hands upon me, but I can feel them easing themselves closer. Seth's eyes dart between the two of them, then rest upon me. "You are accused of witchcraft!" he says, raising his voice so that the last word is yelled. His lips struggle like an earthworm wriggling in a boiling pot. He points a finger towards my chest, then glances at his companions.

Again there is a hint of panic in his eyes, as if this were the climax of a play and they are in danger of omitting the very action that will wring from the audience the applause they crave.

At last a hand comes down upon each of my shoulders. It is a clumsy movement like that a newborn calf makes as its hooves come into contact with the slippery turf.

"Aren't you rather old to believe such nonsense, Seth Butt?"

"If only tragedy did not demand belief, old hag," he says. As though underlining the insult, Jack Power's fingers dig deeper into my shoulder and Joshua's grip becomes tighter.

"What tragedy?" I ask. And for the first time my lips tremble. Now they have overcome their timidity, there is little I can exploit to lever my way to freedom. The rest—what they know, or think they know, how and why Emma Rose betrayed me when it was not in her interests to do so—these are just details. I am caught fast. They will never let me go.

"The double tragedy you know well," Seth shouts, his henchmen gripping me harder and pressing me downwards as if I were struggling—which I am not. "The double tragedy you created."

"I know only of Sara Rose's disappearance," I say feebly. The plainest statement now sounds like the practiced art of deception on my lips. I can sense their minds skipping ahead to so much else they think I must know.

"Villainous witch!" Joshua blurts. There's a curious lack of conviction in his woolly voice despite his choice of words. "You were not content to murder our poor Sara. You had to use Seth's poor nephew as your instrument."

Joshua's hand grasps me harder and he is overtaken with emotion, it seems. Seth's expression changes too; his eyes water and he nods gratefully to Joshua. He struggles to speak and the men on either side hold me attentive while he wrings the words out of himself: "You made him kill the thing he loves. You have cursed him for life."

"We should take her down now," Jack Power breaks in. "Before she casts another spell."

"At once," Seth agrees, pulling himself together.

They turn me around and march me onto the pathway leading down to the settlement. Now and again Joshua or Jack Power wrenches one of my arms as if I were attempting to escape. Seth strides on ahead, swinging his arms like a soldier. But when he sees the clumps of people waiting down below, he gets embarrassed, scratches his head, waits for us three to pass, and then comes up the rear.

Some of the people scatter and disappear into their homes as I raise my head in their direction. Others, like Elizabeth Rose, Emma, and Mary remain huddled together. Elizabeth's delicate frame looks particularly frail. I catch Emma's eye and—would you believe it?— see the hint of a smile. She lays her head slowly on her mother's shoulder. Elizabeth's hand reaches around her daughter's neck and strokes her hair. She pulls Mary tight to her other side. The child sucks her thumb and grips her mother's skirt.

Then, on top of the little mound upon which Seth's house stands, I see a sight that explains everything. Moping with shoulders hunched, kicking pebbles along the ground, is David Butt. The sun is behind him and his face is in shadow, but I can see him glance up at me before he shuffles around the corner of his uncle's house and out of sight.

So Emma may not have given me away, after all. And Sara's body may not even have been found. Is David Butt alone to be my executioner? Is it he who has told of witchery driving him to murder? As I am under guard and he is not, it's clear the people of this settlement must have entirely believed him.

Jack Power hauls my shoulder roughly and I am forced to turn right and ascend a little slope to the tiny schoolhouse which looks out onto the ocean. A group of small children kneeling and playing with stones gape for a moment at our approach, then jump up and run away, scuffing the turf with their shoes. They do not squeal or shout.

We come to the schoolhouse entrance and the men hesitate. We cannot enter three abreast, and the dilemma of whether to go in first and haul me in after, or push me in, then follow, causes a momentary return of indecision. In the end, Jack Power enters and pulls me in after. Joshua lets go for a moment, then bounds in after me and grabs hold of my wrist. Seth clumps in last.

"Tie her up in the chair," orders Seth. "Make sure she's facing the wall."

Jack Power picks up a heap of rope from the floor, while Joshua's two hands guide me uncertainly by the shoulders to a chair opposite the door. He turns the chair around so it's facing the wall and I sit down from tiredness rather than submission. As soon as I do so, the rope is coiled around my chest and shoulders, pulling my spine hard against the back of the chair. I can feel hot breath gushing past me as Joshua and Jack grunt and strain over this task. My shoulders have been strapped so hard my fingers tingle. I stare at the wall in front of me and the thought comes like lightning: The grimy wood, the wormholes, the cross hanging above my head, may be among the last sights I ever view without the imminent terror of death. It is sadness that accompanies this thought, not fear. I must say goodbye to them all—my cabin, my solitude, my medicines, the forest with its echoes and whispers. And I must say goodbye to memories, too. My children, my husband, my mother and father, Thomas Ridley, the playwright so insecure he was hurt by the judgment of a child. All of these people, my constant companions through the years, will die a second time, and this time forever as my recollections are consumed by fire or suffocation. The thought nearly drives me to panic. I'm suddenly aware of my weakness against the thick rope.

"Bring in Simon Rose and the witnesses," murmurs Seth.

"Right away," answers Joshua. I feel his footsteps vibrate along the wooden floor. He closes the door after him and the daylight fades to the muted hues of a prison cell.

CHAPTER TWELVE

I remember how it came upon me suddenly, the knowledge that I really had lost everything. It was a few days after my consignment to this cell. The serving woman, who I now knew as Bess, had given us food, some bread, and meat on a bone. I'd eaten hungrily. So had the playwright. The rat emerged as it usually did at the end of a meal. The playwright began throwing it some morsels of bread he had kept. I had eaten so eagerly that I had forgotten to save any scraps. This fact—my thoughtless greed in robbing myself the little pleasure of feeding our pet—became too painful to endure. I fixed my eyes upon the window and held down tears while in the corner of my vision the playwright threw and the rat caught.

Suddenly I saw myself from the outside, the change that had come over me. Long gone was the forest, and gone was my mother's distracted affection. No more Thomas Ridley with his pale eyes and his red lips. The day used to stretch before me in a rainbow of possibilities. Now someone had blown out the sun and there were only these bleak walls, faces ingrained with misery and dirt, and the all-pervading smell from limbo. All I had to look forward to was the pleasure of feeding a creature I once considered vermin.

Bess had been right to put a cheerful face on things that first day. She knew that in time I would come to appreciate the simple functions life had kept open for me. I began to look forward to seeing her. Her fussy good nature was like a warm blanket over my shoulders, like the mother's comfort I no longer had. I even looked forward to seeing the guard, Gilbert, whose sallow face watched mine through the open doorway still, not with suspicion, which he had every right to feel, but with the ghost of concern. The playwright was a comfort too, though his moodiness disturbed me.

The threat of tears subsided as the last scraps were thrown, but I still felt the deep chill of desperation. I sighed a few times and tried to look as miserable as I could. I had an idea that, as I was thirteen and he was over thirty, he might think it his duty to comfort me. He probably didn't think any such thing and, even if he did, he didn't seem to notice my distress.

I got up, walked over to the window, and curled my fingers around the bars.

"This is the worst," I said out loud. It wasn't a complete thought and I meant to finish it with something like, ". . . day of my life," but I'd caught the playwright's attention sooner than I'd expected, and he interrupted.

"The worst?" he said, finding one last scrap in the straw and throwing it at his friend. "The worst is not so long as we can say, 'This is the worst.'"

I turned around to see his eyes alert and looking up at mine. The rat watched me too. It twitched its nose and descended from its hind legs onto all fours.

"How do you mean?" I asked.

The playwright frowned. I could see he was getting frustrated, so I took a step forward and said, "Yes, I think I know what you mean."

He nodded, encouraged.

"You mean . . . that if you are in a position to say anything, if you are still alive, then it is not without hope."

"Exactly!" he said, delighted.

"That's so true!" I said.

I wasn't nearly as struck by the thought as I pretended to be. It seemed a bit obvious.

"Despair is your worst enemy in here," he said, gazing not at me but at the animal, which now buried its muzzle in its flank, grooming itself after the feast.

"I know," I said, then, not to seem presumptuous, added, "I mean, I think you must be right."

"Well, in that case," he said, pulling his knees to his chin, "what are your plans?"

"Plans!" I repeated with a laugh. "What kind of plans can I make in a prison cell? What are your plans?"

The playwright was motionless for a second, considering.

"There are people working for my release right now. People in the profession."

I went back to my corner and sat down slowly.

"That's not much of a strategy either," I said quietly, not wanting to goad him too much.

He sighed and pursed his lips. "Yet it will work," he replied so casually it was hard not to believe him. "You know why?"

"No."

"Because of the most reliable influence in the world," he murmured, "the balm that eases all sorrow, the comfort that quells all fears. The eternal word."

"What eternal word?" I whispered, feeling on the verge of some mighty revelation.

The playwright smiled. "Gold!" His eyes sparkled, not with mirth but with bitterness. "My plays make money. There are those with vested interests who want them performed. And the politicians who put me here have itching palms. They love money more than they hate my plays." He looked up at me again and gave me a tight grin. "It may be tomorrow. It may be next week, or next month if I'm unlucky, but I am certain of release. Which is why I'm asking you about your own prospects." He smiled at the grooming rat. "Delightful though this brave new world may be with such lovely creatures in it, you need a plan to get yourself out."

I felt my shoulders tighten and the chill return to my stomach.

"I don't have one," I said.

The playwright picked up some straw and dropped it again, then knitted his hands together in a steeple above his knees. "Tell me, is your stepfather rich?"

"Yes, I think so."

"And your mother, did she have money?"

"She had property. Everyone was after it when my father died."

The playwright nodded and looked to the window.

"What I said to you before," he said quietly, "about you being here because they feared your judgment . . ." He hesitated.

"Yes?" I prompted, leaning forward.

"That's probably only part of it."

"What's the other part?"

"Money," he said with a sigh. "Gold again!" He gazed at me intently, as though willing me to absorb some knowledge that had long ago become a part of him. "It's at the bottom of everything," he breathed, his voice trailing to a whisper. "It's the cause of oppression, the currency of love." He raised both palms upwards and tipped them slowly to face the ground; nothing was in them, so nothing fell. But I got the idea. "Your stepfather means to use his son to further his position. The child of a rich man is a precious commodity. His boy can buy him a dowery. He will not be given away for free."

"I know he thought me not good enough for Thomas," I said, looking down and breaking straws with my hands. I was aware the message was more complicated than this, but I allowed myself to slide into a sulk. It felt comfortable too, like a luxury I had denied myself.

"Don't play the fool," the playwright said. "I know you are sharper than that, and you'll need to be if you are to find your way out of here."

"But how do I get out of here?" I asked suddenly, my heart quickening.

I felt the playwright had unmasked me and set me before a mirror. I had imagined myself in love with Thomas Ridley and thwarted in love by my incarceration. But my cellmate had shaken the fancy loose. Thomas Ridley was no more essential to me than a daydream, and the wings of my own ambition were broader than I had painted them.

"You should do something that will utterly convince your stepfather you are no threat to his son's affections, and no impediment to his growing estate."

"How?" I demanded.

The playwright took a deep breath and stared at the floor, considering.

"Telling him will not be enough. You must take yourself out of the picture."

Mr. Ridley and Mr. Jarvis sat close together, their shoulders almost touching. I was in my customary place in this room at the end of the table. Bess and Gilbert had been dismissed. I stood looking directly in front of me, my brow furrowed, my eyes watery with repentance as the playwright had instructed.

"So," said Mr. Jarvis, moving backwards and forwards in his chair like a bull wallowing in a lake, "you see your kind guardian has come in response to your missive." He glanced nervously towards Mr. Ridley, as if unsure of his role in the discussion. "I trust we have taught you enough about obedience to ensure you do not abuse Mr. Ridley's kindness."

Mr. Ridley didn't look at either the governor or myself. He merely swallowed and gazed at the table. Mr. Jarvis glanced at him again. "We have been experimenting with your stepdaughter, Mr. Ridley, trying to discover the degree to which she has been infected by the scourge of witchcraft. Is that not so, young woman?"

"Yes, sir," I replied softly. "I have looked the horrors of corruption in the face. I am ready to repent such wickedness forever, and

pay for my sins with a lifetime of good works, if God wills it so."
My short time with the playwright had given me a strong sense of
drama. My voice was resonant with feeling. My lip trembled as I
spoke, and by the time I had finished speaking, I almost believed
myself.

"Indeed," said Mr. Jarvis, somewhat taken aback. "And what
did you make of our playwright?"

"A mind diseased with wickedness, sir," I replied in quavering
tones, "a soul in the very torment of unrepentance." I felt badly
talking of my cellmate in such a manner, but he had insisted that I
must.

"Well," said the gaoler, brightening. "You can see, Mr. Ridley,
you can see how we work here for the reclamation of our inmates,
no matter how far they have fallen."

"Indeed, sir," Mr. Ridley whispered, his gaze still on the table.

"So," said Mr. Jarvis, shifting and preparing to rise. "I will leave
you together, as you have requested, sir. This is entirely in your
hands and a matter for your own discretion."

The chair scraped against the floor as he rose. He walked to the
exit in silence then, coughing slightly in a gesture of studied dignity,
as he left the room. Mr. Ridley did not lift his gaze from the table
until the governor had closed the door. When his eyes met mine, I
was aware that accusation was trying to burst forth from my face
and show itself. But I relaxed my brow and cheek as the playwright
had advised and I felt the danger pass away.

"You mentioned a convent," he said. It was like a sentence from
the middle of a conversation rather than an introduction. I had to
remember what I said in the letter.

"When I thought of the danger I had put you and your family

through, sir," I said quietly, "I began to think of ways to make some recompense."

"It is an idea," he said quietly, "and there are such convents abroad." He paused for a moment and added carefully, "They follow the church of Rome, you understand."

"But that is why I must go," I said with breathless enthusiasm. "Such an institution would give your honoured family a sense of safety, as I could not easily return. And if I should return to wicked ways," I said, slowing down and clasping my hands together as though struggling with myself—I needed to draw as much attention to the next part as possible; the playwright insisted it was a line that never failed to please— "and you know how weak and fragile is the will of woman, how changeable, how easily distracted from its course—I would nevertheless be far away, cloistered, and unable to cause harm."

Mr. Ridley suddenly stood and turned away from me.

"No one must know," he said quietly. He turned his head slowly until I could see his profile. "There must be no letters, and you must never return."

I had the most curious feeling in my chest. It was as though my heart had swelled and was pushing against my ribs. I had won. I had accomplished what I had set out to do. Yet here, in the very midst of victory, I felt like screaming out in anger. I was merely leaving one prison for another, and this new gaol would be as elaborate as a palace and as impregnable as a fortress. Each one of its bricks would be fashioned from pure deceit.

I trembled in fury, watching the side of this man's face.

"Do you agree?" he asked.

"Never to write to my mother?" I said, as calmly as I could.

"It would be best for us all," he replied. He turned slightly towards me again and, for the first time, I saw fear in his expression. "You don't know how close we all were to damnation," he murmured. "It was a warning."

Now I knew there was something I did not know, something beyond the gold of which the playwright spoke, beyond even the shame of Mr. Ridley's hasty marriage with my mother. My heart thumped hard and my throat felt constricted. I had to know.

"Tell me," I said. "Tell me what you're afraid of and I'll agree to everything."

I didn't care what I promised now. I knew I was on the verge of something and I could not back away.

He stared at me for a moment. All the angular strength was gone from his face, washed away by his anxiety. "I knew your mother before," he said, bowing and resting his knuckles on the table.

"I know you did," I replied, slightly impatient.

"I knew her for many years, many years." The last part was like an echo fading into space. "I knew her before you were born."

He was silent again, but my heart drummed its battle rhythm.

"When you say 'knew,'" I said quietly, "do you mean . . . ?"

"Yes!" he interrupted, bowing again and gritting his teeth. "Yes, that's what I mean."

"So," I said doubtfully. "What has that got to do with me?"

He took his knuckles from the table, stood up straight, and sighed.

"Everything," he said. "It has everything to do with you, and everything to do with you and my son."

Newgate is hardly ever silent. There is constant audible motion from somewhere within its many cells and chambers—doors opening or closing; people yelling, screaming, laughing, arguing; gaolers walking the corridors with jangling keys; stonemasons working. But this, at least in my memory, was one of those rare moments when there was not the slightest sound. I looked into the moist eyes of the man in front of me and, against my will, I understood.

"No," I said with a certainty I did not feel. "It isn't true."

"It might not be true," he said through pursed lips. "But, then again, it might be."

"Your eyes are dark and mine are green."

"Thomas's eyes are pale also, yet I know for certain he is my son. Your eyes prove nothing."

"But I am like my father . . ."

Mr. Ridley raised his eyebrows, then looked to the floor.

"I mean the father who died. I am like him in disposition and taste. We had the same minds, the same interests!"

"All of which can be learned from habit, from the long practice of company and conversation."

"But I would have known," I insisted, suddenly angry. "I would have known if Thomas were so forbidden. My senses would have warned me."

"But you have trained your senses in the bogs and forests of a heathen land," said Mr. Ridley, his voice sharp now. He stood behind the table again, leaning into it as though it were a shield. "The values it has taught you are those of rank bestiality. Your senses would have told you nothing awry because they have long wallowed in evil."

"He is not my brother," I said with conviction. "And you are not my father."

He winced at the last words as though receiving a blow, then he squared his shoulders proudly. "Father or not, I have been severely tested by you. You bring chaos to order, darkness to light. I am not trying to punish you, and I owe you this one chance of redemption. It is my atonement. You must agree to my terms or remain in this place."

There was a pause and his eyes locked on mine.

CHAPTER THIRTEEN

The boards of the schoolhouse floor vibrate beneath me as the witnesses enter. I hear their breathing and the rustle of their clothes as they move, but I cannot catch as much as a single whisper. My arms pull against the ropes again—I can't help struggling, although I know it's futile—and my skin chafes. The wood of the cross on the wall is splintered and its surface disfigured by wormholes. I imagine myself crawling into one of these minute tunnels and disappearing. I laugh suddenly at the idea. Of all the situations I have been in, this is the most absurd. If only I could tell them they are acting like fools, that they should untie me at once and go home or go about their business. Suddenly, I feel a movement and a shadow above my head.

"See how she mocks the holy cross with her laughter," says Seth Butt. His arm reaches over me and takes the cross from the nail. "She will put a curse upon it." The wall above me is now bare and I hear Seth retreat behind me, returning to the group.

"Should we begin with a prayer?" asks someone—I think it must be Joshua.

"We must pray afterwards, when the deed is done," says a man with a soft voice. Though he sounds rather timid, everyone becomes silent as they listen to him. I can taste fear and respect in the air. "First we must recite together the words we learned for our protection."

"Of course," says Seth. "Simon is right."

There is a general murmur of agreement and a pause. Like a wave crashing on the shore, the voices begin, those of men, women, and children interweaving, yet slightly mistimed, like the grinding of pebbles under the incoming tide:

"Lock them out; lock them out. Lock them out forevermore.
"Lock them out; lock them out. Lock them out forevermore."

There is a momentary pause.

"Curse go back; curse go back. Back with double pain and lack.
"Curse go back; curse go back. Back with double fear and flak."

Silence. Someone shuffles his feet. Another person coughs. I stare at the grimy wall. The wood is paler where the cross has stood and wormholes stand out sharply and clearly defined. Again I imagine myself crawling into one of them. This time I stop myself from laughing, though I do not know how laughter could make things any worse.

"Let us hear from our principal witness," comes the soft voice of Simon Rose.

There's a sound of people shuffling to the side, making room. David Butt coughs.

"Don't worry, boy," says Seth. "Tell the truth and no harm will come to you."

There is a hesitation, and then David clears his throat again. "It started when I collected wood for the . . . accused," he begins uncertainly. "I listened to Mr. Simon reading from the gospel on Sunday, how he told us to help those who were less fortunate than ourselves."

There is a rumble of approval behind me.

"I thought about the old woman, Sheila, up on the hill," he continues with more confidence. "I knew she couldn't move around much and I thought how difficult it must be for her to collect her own wood."

"A gracious and Christian thought," says Simon Rose in an encouraging tone.

The ropes are constricting my ribs and making it hard to breathe. It occurs to me to interrupt this foolishness, but I haven't the energy at the moment. The first bead of sweat trickles down my forehead. I calm myself and listen.

"I went and collected wood for her and she asked me to come in and sit down," David continues. "Then she told me that I was in love with Sara Rose and that I should let no one stand in my way."

"And what did you reply?" asks Simon Rose.

"That I loved and honoured my neighbour as the Bible instructed me to, sir, but that nothing else was between us."

"Go on," says Simon quietly.

"And then . . . and then, everything went dark . . ."

"Yes?" Simon's voice is a whisper and the room is suddenly

unnaturally hushed, as if all the spectators were holding their breath.

"And then there was an evil-smelling smoke," says David with some hesitation.

"What colour was the smoke?" asks Simon breathlessly.

"Yellow."

"Sulphur!" a man's voice breaks in. There is a general gasp, half-suppressed.

"Thick yellow smoke curling before my eyes," continues David.

"And what did she say to you?" asks Simon Rose urgently.

"She said, she said, I was no longer to be myself. I was to obey the will of her master, the devil."

A woman shrieks and there is a hubbub—a stamping of feet and a sharp yell. For a moment I fear I will be attacked and killed from behind. My arms strain against the rope as I try to lift my hands to shield my throat from a blade. But then everything falls silent.

"Is she all right?" asks Simon.

"Just fainted," replies a breathless man, possibly Joshua, although I cannot tell for sure.

"Now, David," says Simon with hardly a pause. "What else do you remember?"

There is the vibration of footsteps as the woman who swooned is taken from the building. The door opens and then closes again.

"Everything afterwards was like a dream," David says, his voice suddenly full of wonder. I would never have credited the boy with so much imagination. "I walked down to the wharf one morning as though compelled against my will. I spoke with Sara, but the words were not mine. It was as though someone else had taken hold of my tongue."

"And then?" Simon Rose asks gravely. "What happened then?" The door opens again and someone shuffles back in.

"And then my hands reached out," says the boy, his voice rising to a yell. "They looked like my hands, but some other force outside myself was driving them! I tried to stop it! I screamed at my hands to stop squeezing her neck . . ."

"Enough!" orders Simon. "Enough of that." There is another pause. "And how did you come to be free of it? How did you rid yourself of the devil's influence?"

"I don't remember clearly," comes the reply. "I was in the forest for the day and most of the night as though sleepwalking, then I found myself coming to the town."

"Found yourself hungry and without food," I manage to croak. Despite the pain of the ropes, I find myself chuckling.

There is a moment's silence. I am not sure how far my voice has carried.

"Burn, vile witch!" David yells in my ear. He is close enough for his spittle to land on my neck.

The floor creaks and it seems someone comes to restrain him.

"It's all right, young man, we know how you feel," says Simon. "Tell us what it was that brought you back from Satan."

"It was when I broke into your own house, sir, intent upon I know not what . . ."

"Tell the people," urges Simon patiently.

"In your home, sir, I saw by the rolling light of the moon the silver cross hanging above your hearth. Suddenly, the dreadful nightmare, the evil influence I was under seemed to disappear and I fell to my knees and wept for the blood of my Lord and Saviour."

Simon Rose gives a long, contemplative sigh.

"So, you see," he says at last, his voice little more than a whisper, "though it was my own dear child who perished, I forgive this simple boy." The boards creak to a soft thread and I suspect Simon Rose is placing his comforting hand on David's shoulder. "I can see there was an influence at work upon him, one that none of us can vanquish without God's help."

Simon's audience is so quiet, so focused upon his words, that I wonder for a moment whether they have all suddenly disappeared. But then, as the floor creaks once more, I hear a few murmurs of approval. "This, my friends," Simon continues softly, "is why I am asking that we burn this witch without delay."

And suddenly the world stops. The silence I believed I had been hearing seems like a maelstrom of noise and distraction compared to the icy stillness that now reigns. The breeze has ceased blowing; the birds have paused in mid-flight; the men and women standing behind me have all turned to stone. Burning will be unnecessary, I feel I should tell him: save your firewood—my blood has stopped running of its own accord. I will be dead in a matter of moments anyway.

"Should we not hear what the old woman has to say, Simon?" a lone voice breaks the spell. "So we know we are doing things properly," the dissenter adds hesitantly.

"It is an honourable thought, Joshua," Simon replies, "but you must see the danger. This creature can turn us all towards murder and mayhem with a flicker of her eyelid. There is only one safe course for our wives and children. We must burn the evil from this village before it consumes us all in hellfire."

"He's right," Seth insists. "The case is proven. We must commit her to the flames."

"You would say that," says another, possibly Jack Power. "It's your own nephew who did the killing."

Suddenly, a number of voices are raised and I can hear none distinctly. Seth's harsh tones bark above the rest, his words unclear but his indignation vivid enough. Seven or eight people argue at once. Then, quite unexpectedly, the voices trail away.

I hear Simon sigh. "My friends!" The room becomes hushed again. "My friends!" There is a shuffling of feet. "Don't you know that Satan feeds off discord?"

A few people mutter, but others hiss at them to be silent.

"We will leave the witch under guard and repair to my home. There, as good neighbours in Christian goodwill, we will plan some trial by which we can all satisfy ourselves of the witch's guilt."

"Who shall guard?" asks Seth, as the door opens. There is a great rumble of footfalls as people begin to leave.

"Who will volunteer?" calls Simon.

"David cannot," says Seth. "He may fall under her influence again."

"So may any of us," grumbles Jack Power.

"Father," comes a soft voice I do not recognize, "I'm afraid!"

"Afraid, my chuck!" Simon replies fondly. "But the witch is bound. Her face is to the wall, and she cannot harm us."

"But Father," the girl persists—and now I know it is Emma's voice. Its quality has been altered so effectively by feigned innocence as to be almost unrecognizable—"she may overcome any guard you may leave with her. They may free her and then, in turn, they may bewitch others."

Simon makes a distracted sound, somewhere between fond dismissal and a faint realization.

"The safest thing to do, dear Father, is surely to leave her bound and on her own."

"She's right," mumbles Seth.

"Of course!" exclaims Simon, delighted. "Of course! My clever girl! We must leave her alone. Come on!"

I hear Emma skip on ahead. The men follow more heavily. In a moment the door swings to and closes with a bang. I am left in semi-darkness again.

———

The smell of burning brings me to. I have been dreaming of meadows and butterflies, of forests and the scent of sweet pine. My arms feel quite dead and, when I raise my head, I am facing the worm-eaten wall that my dreams had so joyfully blown away.

I hear a clunk from the door behind me and my heart stirs. Are my executioners approaching? There is another noise and the door creaks open. No voices. No footsteps. My dead arms pull against the rope, but then my whole body seems to collapse into defeat. The door creaks again, slowly, like the bending of an aged tree, then shuts. Soft footfalls approach.

"They've set fire to your house, you know," comes the carefree, confident voice of Emma Rose. "I suppose they had to burn something, poor things, while they're waiting for the main event."

"My house!"

"Yes." She crouches down to the side of my chair and I turn my head to see her grinning face. "It was Father's idea. He likes to keep people happy, and he's very clever at it."

I turn my head away and moan.

"I don't know why you should be worried about your house," she says. "You'll be next, after all, and no one else will want to live there."

I sigh, keeping my head stretched as far away from the girl as possible.

"Do you know what they're going to do with you?" she asks.

"No," I groan.

"That'll be fire too, I know it," she says. "Father loves fire. It's part of his . . . I don't know what you'd call it . . . part of his mystery. He always picks out Bible passages that talk about fire. It's his thing. The men who found him drifting in a boat when he was a baby—you know, my grandfather, and his people—were supposed to have set the boat alight as a kind of *offering*." She says the last word in a deep, portentous voice, then laughs.

A vision comes into my head of scorched driftwood bobbing on the surface of the tide and I feel a curious tug of coincidence somewhere. I shake the feeling from me as I would dry leaves when walking through the woods in autumn.

"No one is supposed to talk about Father being found," continues Emma. "We're not even supposed to know, although everyone does. But when it comes to fire, Father can never resist. You know, I think he feels rather frustrated merely following a religion. I think he'd really rather start one and be the next Moses or Jesus or whatever."

I look away again and Emma pauses. I sense her looking me over closely.

"Do you *mind* about what's going to happen to you?" I turn as much as I can to catch her keen eyes and the ghost of a furrow on her brow. "It probably seems like a stupid question, but if I were you, all old and horrible-looking, I'm not sure I would." She shuffles a little closer and I feel her breath as she speaks. "I mean, it's not really as though you're living for very much, is it? If you were to carry on the way you are, you'll just get older and older and die anyway. This way at least it will be over quickly." I glare at her, not answering. She looks to the floor for a moment. "Tell you what," she begins again, in cheerful tones, "I'll ask you two questions, and if you get the answers right—by right I mean the same answers that I have in my head—I'll cut you loose. How's that?"

She's smiling, her clear green eyes expectant. In her white hand is a small, sharp fish knife.

"Why? Why should I?"

She tilts her head to the side knowingly. "Because, old woman, you're terrified, and you don't want to die."

My eyes lock on hers for a moment and I realize with some surprise that she is right. Despite my weariness, my suffering, and a thousand layers of disillusionment, I mean to live. There are mysteries still to unravel, relationships to understand. There are people—many people—Gilbert, my children, my neighbours, Thomas Ridley, the playwright, my father, even my mother—whose memory I cannot allow to burn.

"Ask your questions."

"Here's the first," she says, then pauses. "If I let you go, would you—old and feeble that you are—be able to survive in the forest without shelter?"

I moan and almost tell her to leave me. Terrified or not, this is more than my final strands of dignity can bear; she is surely only playing with me as a child tortures an insect. But as I catch her eye again I see an intensity in her expression.

"Yes," I say defiantly. "I will survive."

"Correct," says Emma.

She smacks her lips and braces herself. "Now the second question. Listen closely."

I sigh and wait.

"If you did survive in the woods, would you remain in a place where I could find you, and in return for food, render me services as I ask them of you?"

"Yes," I reply quickly, before I have had a chance to think about it.

"Also correct!"

Emma springs forward and slips the knife under the rope holding my left arm. She works with it quickly and the hemp gives way, releasing little clouds of dust as the sheathes burst apart. Suddenly my left side is released and my body sags forward as the coil around my chest loosens. Emma scuttles to the other side and cuts through the rope holding my right shoulder. Both my arms throb, but I stand quickly.

"Hold on!" Emma whispers and runs to the door. She turns the handle and presses her head to the widening crack. "They're still on the hill. I can hear them."

She turns to me and beckons. I hobble towards her, a knot of aches and soreness. She opens the door. "Now, you can escape if you go down between those houses, then along the beach." She points the way. "You can gain the forest from the northern cove. But you must move quickly." She steps out of the way, then grabs my arm. I gasp from the pain; she has touched my rope-chafed skin.

She eases her hand away and almost—I think—apologizes. She just stops herself in time.

"You must tell me where you will be," she whispers.

"There is a beaver pond," I reply, "not far within the forest. Your father used to hunt there."

"He took us there once, yes."

"There is a clearing to the east, and a narrow path leading from it. Take the path and I will listen out for you."

Emma backs away from the door. I slowly ease myself from the stairs onto the turf.

I tramp through the deserted settlement to the beach. Voices of celebration waft down from the hill—yells, the odd shriek, and children singing. The noises are carried upon a wave of softly crackling wood. The afternoon sunshine is dulled by the haze of smoke as I crunch my breathless way along the beach to the northern cove and towards a dark wing of the forest which descends to the shoreline.

CHAPTER FOURTEEN

How long will you have to wait?" asked the playwright. He looked over to the window and frowned at the dying sun.

"Just until they can arrange a passage to France," I answered. "I think they want to make sure that when I leave this prison my journey will be swift and without pause. They want to be certain I'll have no time to change my mind."

My cellmate looked to the floor. "So," he said distractedly. "It won't be long . . . not long. There is constant shipping to France." He picked up a straw and stared off at the window again.

"Maybe I could persuade them to give you a quill and some paper so you can write," I said with a brightness I did not feel. "I'll tell the governor some nonsense about how it helps you exorcise evil thoughts."

The playwright continued to stare at the window and I was about to repeat the offer, when he turned to me. "What?" he said.

Then, "No, there's no need. I'll soon be out myself. The guard passed me a letter earlier."

He pressed his hands into the floor and shifted position. Still, he seemed far away and preoccupied.

"You know something," I said suddenly, "I don't know your name."

He met my eyes this time and smiled. "No, you don't. And I don't know yours."

He wiped his palm on his breeches to clean it of straw and grime. For a moment I thought he would come forward and give me his hand. But he just sat there and looked at me.

"You first," I said.

"Will," he said. He was about to gaze out of the window again, but thought better of it and gave me a tight smile instead.

"I need to know your whole name," I insisted. "I need to tell everybody I once knew the celebrated Will . . . so and so. When you're celebrated around the world like Dante or our own Sir Philip Sidney, I'll tell them I once shared a dismal goal cell with you!"

Will laughed and threw his head back so his crown was hard against the wall, then he sighed deeply, put his hands behind his neck, and drew his head back into position. He looked at me seriously. "You will never need to tell people that, I assure you. I am destined for obscurity."

"Why would you say that?" I demanded. "You write plays that make money, you said so yourself, and you're about to be let out of prison."

"That's just the thing," he said, looking down and picking at the straw. "In prison, you can nurture extravagant ideas about yourself. You can believe yourself immortal and quite set apart from the rest of mankind." He sighed, glanced towards the window once more, then fixed his stare upon his hands like a sculptor examining the tools of his trade. "Once I get out into the world again, I'm just one playwright among many."

"I see," I said quietly. "That's what distracts you."

"Well, partly," he says with a sigh. "What about you? What's your name?"

"Sheila," I told him. "Sheila MaGella before my mother married my stepfather, and I don't want his name."

"You should take whatever name you wish and then live up to it as best as you can," he said. "Sheila MaGella is a fine name and very like a song I have heard during fairs and at street corners." He thought for a moment, narrowing his eyes. "Sheila is an old name for Ireland, I think, and MaGella is like NaGeira which, if I am not mistaken, means 'the beautiful' in the tongue of your country." He gave me a warm smile, not unlike the kind I used to receive from my father, and it comforted me to the core.

"My country?" I exclaimed, but my protest was mild and playful. "My country is England. My father was a servant of the Crown."

"To be English, you must live your life in England. You are a child of the country that mothered you. You breathed Ireland's air and walked Ireland's trails. If Spain were to invade England, if they were to send another vast fleet, and if this one were to prove successful, that turn of events would not render me Spanish, would it?"

"No," I say doubtfully.

"Then you understand we are the land from which we draw our knowledge. No amount of politics and war can change that."

I didn't understand him completely, but I wasn't going to argue now. It was late and our imminent parting was in the air; it made me tingle with uncertainty.

"And being in a French convent will not render you French," he added sombrely and then paused. "Which is why you must promise to escape as soon as you're able," he added with no discernible change in tone. "You must not remain in a nunnery."

"I'm only just breaking free from one gaol," I said, laughing. "You're already plotting my release from another!"

He nodded, but suppressed a smile. "Sheila, there are a hundred ways to make yourself free, and we were not born to be stifled. Life is raging about your ears. You don't want to wake to the realization one day that it is already half over and you have not yet begun. You must not go to the nunnery."

"It is a condition of my release," I said with a sigh. "If I break it they will recapture me and bring me here again, or worse."

"A contract made under duress is no contract at all," he replied, "and a young woman of your wit should know how to remould your identity. You can make sure they do not find you."

I gave a weak laugh. "My life isn't one of your plays, Will. I don't think it's so easy to disappear."

"There is a new world, Sheila, a place where your stepfather and all the governors of all the gaols in England cannot reach."

"And how am I to get to such a place?"

Will paused for a moment and stared at the ground. He was so still that for a moment I thought he must have gone to sleep with his eyes open. But then slowly he drew in his breath.

"The guard who comes to us sometimes . . ."

"Gilbert?"

"Yes. He has a cousin in trade in the New World. In Newfoundland to be exact."

"So?"

"I think he means to go, and soon."

"But I hardly know Gilbert," I said rather feebly, as it was not quite true. What I did know was that Gilbert and I seldom spoke. But that did not mean he was unknown to me, not at all. Through the minutest changes in his stonelike expression, through the myriad tender feelings which I held down in myself, but which rose to the surface anyway each time his stoic presence appeared, I had gotten to know him in ways that required no words. The rhythm of my pulse whispered to me that we were as known to each other as young birds reared in the same nest, as sympathetic in mind and feeling as people who had exchanged a thousand evenings of convivial conversation. It was a familiarity that pulled me to him as a bee is drawn to a flower.

Had I been told I would feel this way for another when the fever for Thomas Ridley was upon me, I would have been horrified. But Thomas Ridley's sand-like hair and his pale-blue eyes had spoken to a freshness in me, a belief in an evergreen spring, and I had now cast off that layer of youth. Gilbert spoke to me of the world as it really was; he delved into the bleakness of things and emerged with something hopeful and true. He was silent compassion in a world of confinement. He was concern in the midst of torment. He was as solid as a church gargoyle and as permanent too. Thomas was a subtle brush stroke in a battle scene of cannon and flame. In my present inner world, he blew away unnoticed, a pale ghost against the harsh reality of day.

"Well, he knows you," said Will, attempting to suppress a smile for the second time, this time not so successfully.

"He asked you to speak for him?" I prompted.

"Not exactly, but I felt that he meant to."

The knowledge made me breathless for a moment. I thought of Gilbert and the New World, and I could hear the crackle of burning and the crash of falling glass. I had made a decision. My nunnery was burning.

———

Sometimes the whole of life seems like an escape gone disastrously wrong. Every time the jaws of imprisonment, death, or religious orders have opened to take me, I have eluded them. And what is my reward? A safe and comfortable home full of laughter and love? A paradisal garden of verdant, plump leaves, warm sunshine, and clean, running water? No. The final consequence of all my amazing luck and agility is an old woman scrambling up a forested hill with the stench of her burning home in her lungs. A woman without husband or child, a crone who will hereafter rely on a malignant child for her survival.

I pause again, weighing all this as a farmer might weigh his last grain after a long drought. Now I am under cover, there is no sense in rushing. These people know nothing of the woods that surround them, and I know everything. A weasel scurries past and a crow flaps its wings in the branches overhead. The sun is sinking and dusk makes me calmer. I recite to myself the words of the green man. *The forest is yours,* he said. *While the woods embrace you, no spirit or beast can harm you, no strangers or neighbours smite*

you, no dank ague infect you. When death lies all around you, the
leaves and boughs protect you.

The rhythm of the words soothes me as before, but there is an
undercurrent of disquiet. For the first time I feel something is missing. I remember how I felt tricked by my father's death, how it
seemed that the man of the forest had misled me when I realized
that the words addressed only me and not my family.

Was there some other loophole? Some other omission that
might deceive me into believing I am safe? The phrases run through
my mind like a breeze through rippling foliage: *No spirit or beast
can harm you, no strangers or neighbours smite you* . . . For the
second time in my life it sounds too specific. *Spirit* . . . *beast* . . .
strangers . . . *neighbours* . . .

I have no idea why I should be doubting these things now. I feel
like a bird who, sensing a change in the wind, prepares for sudden
flight without any detailed knowledge of the danger it faces. It is
intuition only that ruffles my feathers, yet I have learned to pay
attention. Something happened in that schoolroom. Something was
said to cause this shift in the breeze. I touch the bark of the nearest tree with my fingertips and hold my head very still. I wait for a
recent memory to return.

I hear Emma's taunting voice as she crouches on the floor
beside my chair. They took the baby from the boat, she said, and
then . . . yes, then she said they "set the boat alight as a kind of
offering." She had spoken the last word in a deep, portentous voice
before breaking into laughter. And what came into my mind when
I heard this story?

A vision of scorched driftwood bobbing on the surface of the
tide. I knew this was a discovery even while I shrugged it off. And

now as I prepare for the implications to seep in, a rogue thought slips into my mind before I can lower the drawbridge against it: *So I have not been as alone as I thought all this time. I have not been stranded from all my relatives.* This is why the words of the green man no longer make me feel safe! *Spirit . . . beast . . . strangers . . . neighbours . . .* Simon Rose is none of these. Simon Rose is my grandson.

Easing myself down on the coarse grass, I gaze up at the pines towering above me. They trail old man's beard like seaweed from their branches. *Nothing is proven! Nothing is proven!* Yet my search for the child, Matthew, comes back into my mind. I scour the beach once more, calling his name. I skirt the rims of the forest until the tree trunks are a blur. I look again under the woodpile. Then I remember what I have so often tried to forget: Katherine ducking from the pirate's blade, disappearing under the rim of the boat, then pushing herself off from the side and running from the man, her toes skimming the waters. Why was she standing by the boat? The forest would have been safer, I had told her that. *But in a forest,* an answer returns like an echo, *a motherless child would perish. Placed in a boat, under a blanket, there is always the chance of rescue.*

Inwardly I watch again as the boats drift out of the bay and the pirate ship sails towards the horizon. The dark branches loom knowingly overhead, sages of the forest. *Is it cruelty that imparts this knowledge to me now? What else can the nature gods and goddesses have in mind?* I remember poor Will's play, how the ending hinged upon the idea that a man was "not of woman born" if he was taken by surgery before the time. How little I respected the idea, yet how pertinent such trickery has become!

At last I have an answer for John Rose's behaviour. He knew he had stolen my kin, or, at very least, suspected it. That is why he shuffled so shamefaced at my door when delivering supplies. That is why he filled my grandson with terror regarding the old woman on the hill. Old as I am, I feel a rebel blood stirring, screaming for justice and revenge. What law exists for such cases? And what authority is there to enforce it?

In an instant I know the answer to both questions: *none but myself.*

CHAPTER FIFTEEN

It was close to midnight when I was released. The courtyard was empty, as Gilbert said it would be, and my stepfather's servant, the same white-faced woman who had brought me here, sat in the waiting coach.

Sometimes it is much easier to do what is expected, even when you desperately want to do otherwise. Newgate had been my whipping post and, despite myself, the first crisp taste of the midnight air found me shivering with remorse. I saw the expression on the white-faced woman as she looked at me and nodded; it wavered between censoriousness and approval, as though both emotions normally kept in reserve were ready for unfurling, according to how I behaved. Quite unexpectedly I found this meant something to me. There was still someone in the outside world to whom my actions counted, even if it were only for a half-hour coach ride to the London docks.

I thought of Will, Bess, and Gilbert. What of *their* expectations? I asked myself.

But Will, Bess and Gilbert were not the real world. None of them had a connection to anything I had known outside the walls of Newgate. As I climbed into the coach, I felt that my prison friends might fall away from me like gaol dust and spiral off into the night with the first gust of wind.

I think we all knew this would happen. Breaking away was designed to be hard, so we had left nothing to chance.

The coach jolted into movement and my heart picked up its pace. Shadows obliterated the moonlight as the wheels rumbled us through the courtyard entrance. The white-faced woman didn't say anything to me, and I was glad; I had so little breath, she would have suspected something had I been forced to speak.

The carriage turned the corner, then stopped. My companion sighed quietly and drummed her fingers on her lap. There was a yell from the driver; the coach rocked once, then twice. It seemed a long time that we waited in silence. I was beginning to worry and the white-faced woman turned and stared directly at me. Was it fear or accusation in her face?

At last the door swung open and a masked man appeared. He grabbed my arm and pulled me from the coach. My feet stumbled on the steps—I was trying not to act like I expected it—and then I was pulled with some force down a section of road, my footsteps clattering through the night. We ducked into a long alleyway, jumping over drunks and vagrants as we ran, then emerged on the other side. Gaining a doorway at last, Gilbert hauled me deep into the shadows and ripped off his mask. We both stood against the wall, breathing hard. Tears of exertion stung in the cool air and I could taste the blood of tiny burst veins in my mouth. I found laughter rising between breaths. It was all too much; the mad escape, the sudden change in my status from convent girl to fugitive. It was too deranged even for the stage.

"I must hide you quickly," said Gilbert.

"Yes," I replied, and as I thought I heard reproach for my laughter in his tone, I added, "I'm sorry."

"You must trust me, Sheila," he said.

I couldn't see his face at all, but his voice took me by surprise with its tenderness. I had the sensation I had fallen through a seemingly endless night—a night of sorrow and death, confinement, and deception—and that the falling was over. I was landing upon a bed of soft feathers. I felt that, despite the tribulations that lay ahead—voluntary confinement until it was safe to walk abroad, an ocean voyage through perilous seas—there was some comfort.

It was many hours to dawn and I knew there were doubts and worries to plague me yet. But the instinct which was central to it all, that this man who expressed so little would in time come to mean so much, I would never seriously question. I was leaping into darkness again, and I was growing to love the uncertainty.

———

A thin cloud skims through the crescent moon and the breeze stirs around me, shimmering the leaves. Whether I'm protected or not, they will not catch me tonight. I have heard nothing to suggest a proper search is going on. There have been voices in the settlement and voices by the smouldering remains of my house. They have kept to the open ground, it seems, afraid of night and the forest—afraid of me.

I am at the edge of the forest now, gazing down upon the settlement. Windows burn sleeplessly but nobody stirs without. It is past midnight. How smug the Rose home looks! I think of the many nights John Rose must have slept soundly with the growing child he had stolen asleep in its crib. I remember the slow, deliberate fashion with which the boy moved when he threw dust into my eyes. The child must have felt it a justified act.

I look again at the sliver of moon hanging over it all, its austere light skimming over the crags and cliffs to the south, kissing the ripples of the ocean, catching the damp boughs of the Rose home. All nature is mute, it seems; indifferent to theft, careless of slander. Though I communed through the decades with the trees and the wind, no whisper ever came to me of the crime.

My eyes fall upon the Rose door and, at that very instant, it comes open. There is no noise and I strain to see if I am mistaken. The door opens wider and a figure emerges. It is Simon Rose; he turns softly, easing the door shut. My blood quickens. *This is him—Matthew!* I tell myself this, but I cannot connect the thought to my heart. He is a patch long-fallen from a mended cloth. I cannot weave him back in a second.

Simon Rose makes his way—in silence, treading gently—up the hill towards the ruins of my house. I feel a tug in my chest pulling me forward to meet him. I resist, at first. But the lure is too great and I find myself skirting the woods as quietly as I can to get closer to the site of my former home, closer to the man who was once my grandchild.

Simon's strides are long, his head bowed as he nears the spot. I am breathless from the trek and from the effort of keeping my footfalls silent. Hidden only a thicket from the clearing where the ash and debris lay, I daren't move. Simon stands over the site, his fists turned in upon his lips in an attitude of deep thought. He sighs, raises his head, drops his hands, and turns full circle. Then quietly, too quietly to be sure, he seems to say my name: "Sheila."

He looks up in the direction of the woods where I stand. I cannot see his expression as the moonlight is behind him, but I sense he is searching. I know he won't be able to see me and I make sure I do not move.

"Sheila," he says again. And this time I am certain.

Is there a reason I should not reply? Apart from the obvious, that is. I try to imagine Simon Rose jumping on me, pinning me to the ground, and calling his cohorts below. It doesn't seem possible and I realize there is no danger.

"What do you want?" I find myself saying. My voice is firmer than I imagined it would be.

His feet move suddenly against the gravel and for a second I think I was wrong; he really does mean to attack me. But then as I hear a sharp intake of breath, I sense the real reason for his sudden movement. He is frightened.

"Safety," he replies, his voice quavering. "Safety for my daughters and my wife."

He stands motionless in the light breeze. I see only his dark outline against the moonlit hill which rises slightly, then dips away behind him. I stay in the thicket.

"I'm no threat to your wife and children," I say. "I am no threat to anyone."

His head bows slightly. He doesn't know what to say. He is certain I am malignant; I have told him I am not. There is nothing but insult and recrimination between us now, and he is too afraid to go this road.

I decide to open things up. What have I to lose, after all?

"Your father told you lies, Simon Rose," I say quietly.

I can hear his shock in the silence, and I see his shoulders move as though I have caused him to shudder.

"You ungodly serpent!" he whispers so quietly I'm not sure I'm intended to hear. But all my senses are acute for my age. I see and hear most things.

"If I am a serpent, then hear you the truth, Simon Rose." I see him glance around himself, wondering about the quickest escape, so I hurry. "Your father told you stories about me for a reason. The boat in which you were found—the boat they burned—belonged to my husband." He backs away slightly, then crouches to the ground. "And you were placed there by my daughter while we were under attack from pirates. Brace yourself, Simon Rose. The ungodly serpent you spurn is your grandmother."

The last word is lost in Simon Rose's desperate yell as he springs to his feet, having hurled something—a burned piece of wood perhaps—into the forest. He misses me by a long way. "You witch!" he shouts. He crouches down and picks up something else. "We should have burned you when we had the chance!"

I say nothing in case my voice gives him a clue as to where I am. I'm not afraid, just tired, just weary of playing games with rules that stipulate that I cannot win. I'm tired of living near frightened fools and having to negotiate around their fear.

Did Simon Rose even hear the word 'grandmother' through his yell? I'm not sure. Either way, as I watch his shoulders heave and his throwing hand ready itself, I realize I've lost hope for my Matthew, given up on him before his reclamation has even begun.

Simon continues to scan the dark woods. I do not move. Eventually he murmurs something, drops his weapon, and scuffs through the ashes like a child. Then he trudges off down the hill, turning back once or twice as though he believes some beast might suddenly rush at him from out of the darkness.

The faint thud of the Rose door echoes through the night and the words of the playwright come back to me. "A crime that curses generations to come," he had called the murder in Macbeth. I wonder at John Rose's forty-year-old deception and the children of disorder it seems to have bred. "Monsters of the deep," Will might have called them.

Is this true about Emma too?

———

The forest smells sweet today. Warm water trickles from the leaves and scatters tiny droplets into the breeze. The rain left off more than an hour ago, and I can feel the sun heating the earth in that mysterious way it does even through a canopy of branches.

Emma is different in the last day or so. Older, it seems. There was no glee when she told me of her mother's miscarriage, although she admitted it suited her purposes. When she gave the bread to me and I started eating, I saw a curious look come into her face. She suppressed it quickly enough when I caught her eye. I couldn't call it pity, not knowing her as I do. More like unhappiness—an awareness of things not being right when a crone lives out the last of her days exposed to the elements because her community has burned down her home. She has learned to be sensitive to discomfort, and sensitivity is, after all, the mother of pity.

Or perhaps I was wrong about her from the start. Perhaps her wickedness was too extreme to begin with. Maybe now I'm seeing the first few cracks in her mask. In all manner of things, the woman might outstrip the girl. But she has not lost her ambition. She is determined to prevent another heir, and when I asked for a short stretch of rope and told her the reason, she brought it to me in less than an hour. The plan is for her to return once I have made a knot and cast my spell. Then she will secret the knotted rope under her parents' bed.

I stoop and pick up the wet rope. Simon Rose richly deserves his knot of impotence, but I am not sure I will go through with it. I have been listening more intently of late to the sound the breeze makes as it shifts through the leaves, and I have felt my thoughts merging with these subtle movements. At these times I have felt that, however much I wish to punish the Rose family, there is something wrong with the plan.

I stand, the wet rope still in my hand, and make my way around some cranberry bushes towards the clearing. The finches no longer disperse when I approach. This time I even feel the tiny wind from their wings as they hover and duck around the leaves.

I remember how I blamed the green man once for misleading me and not protecting my father. But now I think I misunderstood. The forest does not act; it waits and opens its arms for those who approach it. We may draw our healing powers from the woods as we draw water from the well. But it is passive and does not intrude upon the business of women and men.

My fingertips touch the bark of an aspen as I come into the clearing. The stream nearby sends soft, bell-like chimes into the atmosphere, echoing and multiplying like too many minstrels playing at once. I stand still and listen for a long time, and I feel part of myself dancing somewhere far away to its fanciful, fractured melodies.

One day soon I will die, I realize, and the thought is a happy one. When I was young I heard old people pronounce they are looking forward to death, and I thought them liars. But this is different, or so it seems to me. My spirit is no longer entirely within me. I think of the green man I knew in Ireland, and wonder if this is how he began. Did he also roam the forest in some forgotten century? Did his spirit merge with the forest, then fade into the leaves and boughs as his body fell and the insects came?

My hand opens and the rope drops to the ground. I know what my answer to Emma must be. Let Elizabeth teem more children into the world if she must. It is not my job to stop her, and the cycle of life must go on. The Roses can shed their mendacity when they may.

I move through the clearing and back into the thicket. I feel lighter already, having made my decision, and I breathe in an air of such sweetness I think my senses have taken flight. I can taste the bitterness of the green and unripe cranberries too, and I can hear the steady beat of a moth's wing on the opposite side of the clearing. I turn to see, wondering whether my vision has become as sharp as my hearing and taste—and there it is, a white moth, beyond the open space, deep in a thicket, scooping some mysterious honey from a dripping leaf. But halfway between the insect and me, in the middle of the clearing, there is a curious sight—an old woman curled in the grass, her eyes open, a length of rope near her hand. I think of the crone, her suffering and her joys, and I realize with only the faintest bump of surprise that she is me.

As I turn and continue, I carry her memories, her loves and dislikes, but they do not weigh upon me as they weighed upon her. I am the woman of the forest now. I am formless and infinite and I can shed my sorrows at will. Drifting further into the woods, I feel the girl Emma's progress as she makes her way through the trees towards the clearing. I feel the touch of her footfalls as a bear might feel an ant tickling its way through her fur. The girl glimpses the body in the clearing and runs frantically through the final stretch of long grass. She draws close and falls on her knees. And—see, I was right!—there are tears spilling onto her cheek, and she lets out a long howl, not of frustration or annoyance, but of grief.

I return and hover over her shoulder for a moment and I hear the leaves around us whisper my thoughts. *The forest, my girl, is yours,* they say in gentle, rustling melodies. *While the woods embrace you, no spirit or beast can harm you, no strangers or neighbours smite you, no dank ague infect you. When death lies all around you, the leaves and boughs protect you.*

I see her turn, breathlessly scanning the leaves, taking in the words. She stifles her last moans and stares wide-eyed into the forest—not a monster after all.

I let her feel me for a moment longer, then glide into the thicket again. Mosquitoes dart around me and earthworms wriggle below. I hear the slow hiss of sap beneath the bark and the oozing of sweet waters as they seep up through a thousand roots. Nature rings with a constant harmony of celebration. At last, the music tells me, at last, you have come home.

Acknowledgements

I would like to thank publisher Garry Cranford for encouraging me to write this book, Marnie Parsons for her astute editing, Jerry Cranford for thoughtful suggestions, and the team at Flanker, especially Margo Cranford, Laura Cameron, Brian Power, and Bob Woodworth, for being enthusiastic about this story. Thanks to the Newfoundland and Labrador Arts Council (NLAC) and the City of St. John's for their support. Special thanks, as always, to my wife, writer Maura Hanrahan.

PAUL BUTLER is the author of the novels *Easton's Gold* (Brazen Books, 2005), *Easton* (Flanker Press, 2004), *Stoker's Shadow* (Flanker Press, 2003), which was shortlisted for the 2004 Newfoundland and Labrador Book Awards, and *The Surrogate Spirit* (Jesperson Publishing, 2000). Butler has written for many publications in Canada including *The Globe and Mail*, *The Beaver*, *Books in Canada*, *Atlantic Books Today*, and *Canadian Geographic*. He has a regular film column with *The Social Edge* e-zine and has contributed to CBC Radio regional and national. A graduate of Norman Jewison's Canadian Film Centre in Toronto and a winner in the Newfoundland and Labrador Arts and Letters competition (2003 and 2004), Butler lives in St. John's. His website is www.paulbutlernovelist.com.